HUNTER

TWILIGHT FALLS #3

A.M. SALINGER

COPYRIGHT

Hunter (Twilight Falls #3)

ISBN: 978-1-9162270-1-9

www.AMSalinger.com

Editor: www.ElfwerksEditing.com

Cover Design: A.M. Salinger

CHAPTER 1

THE MUSIC THUMPED IN HUNTER THOMSON'S EARS AND throbbed pleasantly against his skin. He drummed a hand lightly against his arm as he waited for his order, his fingers matching the beat of the pop song blaring from the club's speakers. He flashed a smile at the girl who brought him his beer, turned, and leaned his back against the bar.

His gaze roamed the dance floor a few feet from where he stood. It was packed with hot, writhing men. A dry smile curved his lips as he brought the bottle to his mouth and took a sip of the cold beverage.

Well, hot writhing men is what I came here for.

His eyes found the couple on the far left of the sunken stage. Hunter's smile turned into a full-blown grin.

Irritation danced briefly on Tristan Hart's face when he met Hunter's amused stare. The man working up a sweat against Tristan seemed oblivious to their exchange; Dan Flynn was already on his fourth drink and focused on his mission for the night. Which was apparently to get in Tristan's pants and ride him till the cows came home.

Hunter could tell from the subtle way Tristan was avoiding full body contact with Dan that he wasn't interested. He knew Tristan would never have accepted Dan's invitation had he known the guy would start hitting on him the moment they walked through the doors of the hottest new gay club in L.A. The fact that Dan had told him to bring a friend to the opening night had evidently lured Tristan into thinking his client wasn't interested in him.

Hunter could hardly blame the poor man.

With his quiet brown eyes, rugged good looks, and muscular, tattooed body, Tristan was a picture of understated masculinity. Not only was he hot, his ability to fix any motorcycle and sports cars that landed in his garage made him one of the most sought-after mechanics in the state. It also regularly brought a line of men and women to his door who wanted to get his hands on more than just their hoods.

All evidence pointed to the fact that Tristan's latest client was one such man. Unfortunately for Dan, the sexy mechanic made it a rule never to mix business with pleasure.

Had Hunter not known Tristan since they were practically in diapers, he might have been tempted to have a taste of the guy himself.

Except we're both tops, so that would definitely not have worked out.

Hunter let his gaze wander over the crowded club. It

wasn't everyday he came to L.A. for a night on the town and he was determined to make the most of it.

Having two of his close friends recently get shacked up had made him antsy. It had also been a few months since he'd hooked up with anyone and he very much wanted to come somewhere other than his own hand tonight.

Besides, I have a reputation to keep up. I can't be Twilight Falls' most notorious bad boy when I haven't seen any action other than my own fingers lately.

A man caught Hunter's interest a moment later. Blond, blue eyes. A body that showed he liked to work out. The stranger's mouth curved up as he studied Hunter from where he stood amidst a large group, his expression telling Hunter he liked what he was seeing too. Hunter's lips tilted in an answering smile.

Someone stepped in his line of sight.

Hunter shifted to try and catch the blond's attention. The man blocking his view moved too.

Irritation darted through Hunter.

The guy looming over him was wearing neatly pressed cream chinos, a navy shirt with a red-rimmed collar that matched his two tone dress shoes, and a dark blue blazer. The top three buttons of the shirt were open, exposing an expanse of toned, tanned flesh.

"Can I get through?"

Hunter blinked.

The man's voice was like whisky poured over rough velvet.

He looked up and met a pair of arresting hazel eyes set in a chiseled face blessed by the gods.

The man arched an elegant eyebrow, his expression patient and seemingly heedless of the interested stares he was drawing. He had a good couple of inches on Hunter's own six foot-two.

"The bar?" the stranger added slowly, as if addressing a dimwit.

Hunter flushed and stepped away from the counter. "Er, sure."

The man's cologne filled Hunter's nose as he slipped past and took his place. He smelled of pine and evergreens, like the forests of Twilight Falls.

Hunter stared at the stranger's wide back. It was clear from his charismatic appearance and expensive clothes that he was loaded.

A hand landed on Hunter's shoulder, startling him. He looked around.

It was the blond he'd been eyeing up.

"Hey," the guy said warmly.

"Hey, yourself," Hunter replied with a smile, firmly squashing his burgeoning interest for the man at the bar.

He's not my type, anyway.

The blond indicated the sunken stage. "Wanna dance?"

A teasing grin lit up Hunter's. "I gotta warn you. I have killer moves. Think you can keep up?"

The blond chuckled. He leaned in and whispered hotly in Hunter's left ear.

"I've got some killer moves of my own."

Hunter's dick perked with interest as the blond's breath washed across his skin. The guy took his hand and led him to the dance floor.

Three songs and another beer later and Hunter was

feeling buzzed. He and the blond had definite sexual chemistry; he could tell he would be coming in the guy's hand, mouth, or ass tonight.

"Wanna go somewhere quieter?"

Hunter followed the blond's gaze.

He was looking at a dimly-lit corridor leading to the restrooms.

Hunter masked a frown. He'd hoped they'd be going back to the hotel he and Tristan had booked for the night. A quickie in a public toilet wasn't really his thing.

"It's not what you're thinking," the blond said mysteriously, as if he'd guessed Hunter's thoughts.

Hunter arched an eyebrow. "It's not?"

The blond grabbed his arm. "Come on."

Hunter scanned the club for Tristan as he headed for the restrooms with the blond. He found his best friend with his inebriated client at the bar on the other side of the floor.

Tristan caught his eyes. "Everything okay?" he mouthed.

Hunter nodded and gave him a reassuring wave.

The club's restrooms were stark and clean. They were also thankfully empty bar a handful of men.

One of them was the blond's friend, a guy with dark hair and eyes.

"You brought him," the man said with a grin.

A sinking feeling blossomed in the pit of Hunter's stomach at his expression.

"What's going on?" Hunter asked the blond guardedly.

Blondie smiled at him, his face relaxed despite Hunter's cool tone.

"We thought you'd be a good fit for us."

Hunter suppressed a grimace. *Great.*

He studied the dark-haired guy. "Are you his partner?"

"I am."

"I'm sorry, but I'm not into threesomes," Hunter said gruffly.

Blondie trailed a teasing hand down Hunter's chest all the way to the buckle of his jeans and beyond. "Are you sure? 'Cause you look pretty turned on to me."

Hunter grabbed Blondie's wrist as he stroked his way back up his erection.

"I was, when I thought it'd be just you."

The door to the restrooms opened. Hunter swallowed a curse when he saw the guy who entered.

It was Hazel Eyes from the bar.

The man stopped and looked at them curiously. "Am I interrupting?"

Hunter recovered his senses first. "No, you aren't." He turned to Blondie and his partner. "Like I said, I'm not interested."

Blondie pouted. "That's a shame. I was really looking forward to having a sex sandwich with you."

Hunter stared, not certain he'd heard right. "Excuse me?"

Hazel Eyes turned away and started washing his hands at the sink, but not before Hunter caught the sparkle of amusement in his gaze.

"You know, where one of us fucks your mouth while the other pounds your ass," Blondie explained blithely.

Hunter's jaw dropped open. He caught a glimpse of Hazel Eyes's reflection in the mirror above the row of sinks. The guy's lips were pinched tight and his shoulders were shaking slightly. Outrage shot through Hunter.

Is that asshole laughing at me?!

"I'm sorry to disappoint you," he told Blondie and his partner icily once he'd regained his composure, "*again.* But I'm a top, so nobody is going anywhere near my ass."

Blondie's eyes widened. "Oh, wow." He paused, a moue twisting his mouth. "Are you sure? 'Cause you kinda give off a bottom feel."

"Positive," Hunter growled.

"Oh well, your loss, I suppose," Blondie murmured. "Come on, Jeff, let's get out of here."

Hunter watched wordlessly as the pair exited the restrooms. He blew out a sigh, raked a hand through his hair, and headed for the door.

"You sure you should be going out like that?"

CHAPTER 2

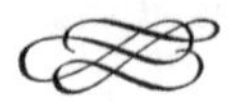

THEO MILLER WATCHED THE MAN FREEZE AS HE STARTED TO reach for the door handle. He lowered his hand and twisted on his heels.

Stormy gray eyes cut to Theo. The guy frowned.

"What do you mean?"

Theo suppressed the chuckle working its way up his throat and did his best to look solemn. He didn't think the man would appreciate his amusement.

"You know?" Theo waved a hand vaguely south of the stranger's belt buckle. "Like *that*."

A flush of color bloomed on the man's cheekbones when he realized Theo was talking about his erection.

Mighty fine cheekbones they are too.

Theo would be lying if he said he hadn't noticed the stranger when they were at the bar earlier. Though the man was dressed pretty casually for the club, his striking face and confident bearing made him stand out from the crowd.

It was clear he was utterly comfortable in his own skin and his sexuality.

Admiration darted through Theo as they eyed each other across the washing area.

The stranger was facing him boldly despite his arousal.

Theo could tell the guy wasn't used to backing down from anything, which intrigued him even more. It wasn't just the man's face that was to his liking.

Though not overtly brawny, it was clear from the stranger's physique that he took great care of his body. The smoothly defined muscles Theo could spy through his jeans and T-shirt made him want to peel the guy's clothes off and find out if they were as nice as they looked.

And that ass is something else.

Theo's fingers twitched slightly as he imagined wrapping his hands over the nicely rounded, tight globes he'd spied strutting on the dance floor a short while ago. The guy sure knew how to move to the music, his sultry expression matching the wicked way he'd rocked the songs pounding through the club.

The stranger seemed to come to some kind of decision. He closed the distance between them, leaned a hip against the sink, and raised an eyebrow. He raked Theo slowly from his head to his toes and back again, his silver gaze daring as he met Theo's stare.

"Why, are you proposing to do something about it?"

Theo blinked, surprised. He swallowed a grin.

His body isn't the only sassy thing about him.

Theo moved until he stood toe-to-toe with the

stranger, forcing him to look up. He could tell the guy wasn't pleased by their height difference.

"Would you like me to?" Theo murmured.

The man's pupils flared in surprise. He licked his lips nervously.

The sight of the pink, moist flesh darting in and out of the stranger's mouth and the flash of white teeth he glimpsed almost drew a groan from Theo.

Shit. That's sexy.

Theo didn't know what possessed him in the next instant. He raised a hand and traced the man's plump lower lip with his thumb, wiping away the trace of dampness he found there.

"So, what's it gonna be, Gray?" he said huskily.

The man's eyelashes fluttered as he blinked, clearly flustered despite his brave expression.

"Hunter," he blurted, his breath washing hotly across Theo's finger.

Theo's dick thickened at the sensation. He angled his head closer, a little stunned by how brazen he was being. Something about this guy just flipped all his buttons, in a hot and dirty kind of way.

"What?"

The man shivered at the question, dark pupils dilating in a sea of smoky gray. There were only a scant few inches separating their mouths.

"My name is Hunter." His gaze grew heavy-lidded as it dropped to Theo's lips.

Damn.

~

HUNTER DIDN'T KNOW WHO MOVED FIRST.

One minute, Hazel Eyes was edging him on, the next their mouths were glued together in a torrid kiss. Desire stormed through Hunter as the man shamelessly probed his lips open. A wave of dizziness swept over him when their tongues clashed hungrily a heartbeat later. Hunter's hands found the stranger's broad shoulders, his fingers sinking into firm, warm flesh as he clung on for dear life.

Holy crap, he's a good kisser!

He was dimly aware of the guy guiding him to the back of the restrooms and around the corner to a stall at the far end. The sound of the metal door clattering open and closing behind them reached him hazily above the sound of blood pounding in his ears.

A small part of Hunter's brain told him he needed to stop. The last time he'd had sex in a public toilet, he'd barely been past the legal age of drinking.

His lower half, however, had other thoughts on the matter.

Though he'd very much wanted to find his release in the comfort of his hotel room tonight, his dick was doing press-ups inside his jeans and he was dying to deliver it from its tight confines.

A throaty groan rumbled out of him when Hazel Eyes did just that, his long fingers unbuckling Hunter's belt swiftly before he slid his zipper down and dipped his hand inside his boxers. A hiss of pleasure left him as the stranger palmed his cock and gently pulled it free before backing him against the wall.

Hunter stiffened slightly. He was used to being in charge under these kinds of circumstances. It unnerved him how easily he was letting this guy take control of the situation.

Hazel Eyes let go of his mouth and leaned away slightly, his heated gaze dropping to where he was touching Hunter intimately. The tender expression on his gorgeous face scattered Hunter's anxious thoughts to the four winds.

"Theo." The man caressed Hunter's erection lightly, as if it was the most precious thing in the world.

Hunter sucked in air, too focused on the sinful feeling of the guy's hand on his sensitive member to pay much heed to anything else.

"My name." Intense hazel eyes met Hunter's own dazed ones. "It's Theo."

Hunter's belly contracted with a spasm of pleasure and something else.

Oh. His eyes get greener when he's excited.

A clink sounded. Hunter looked down and saw Theo unzip his own pants. He swallowed when he saw the enormous erection Theo unleashed seconds later.

"You're big," Hunter blurted.

Theo stared. A sexy chuckle escaped him in the next instant. "I'm going to choose to take that as a compliment."

Hunter shuddered when Theo wrapped one large hand around both their dicks and started rubbing, his movements skillful.

"Fuck, that's good!" Hunter mumbled.

Theo took his mouth in a passionate kiss as he gave them both an expert hand job, his breaths leaving his nose in sharp pants, color staining his cheeks a dull pink under the light illuminating the cubicle.

Hunter curled his fingers in Theo's thick, dark hair and returned the kiss greedily, his body straining toward the man who was pleasuring him, seeking closer contact.

Theo parted Hunter's legs with his right thigh, clasped Hunter's left knee with a powerful hand, and hooked it around his own leg, pressing their bodies together. Hunter moaned, stunned that Theo had done exactly what he'd been hungering for.

Theo let go of his mouth, nipped his jawline with strong white teeth, and lowered his head to nudge Hunter's chin up. Hunter gasped when Theo's hot lips found his throat. Theo rained scorching kisses across his feverish skin before finding the pulse at the base of his neck. He started a seductive bump and grind with his hips while he sucked on Hunter's flesh and kneaded their swollen cocks with a firm hand.

The metal partition they were up against rattled loudly.

Theo stopped, his grip tightening on their erections in a way that sent sparks exploding across Hunter's vision.

Hunter's head reeled when Theo wrapped an arm around his waist, twisted around, and backed him against the tiled wall of the cubicle, his thigh still firmly wedged between Hunter's.

"That's better," Theo said huskily. "Wouldn't want the whole world to know what we're doing in here."

Hunter's rationality dissolved into nothingness as Theo resumed his sexy thrusts, his movements indicating exactly what he wanted to do to Hunter while he stroked their stiff dicks briskly.

Pleasure sent bolts of whiteness shooting across Hunter's mind. He could feel his orgasm building in throbbing waves in his belly and thighs. His balls tightened and his ass spasmed when Theo flicked a lazy thumb across the head of his leaking cock.

"Oh, Jesus!" Hunter panted. He fisted his hands in Theo's hair and bucked his hips hard against Theo's. "I'm so close!"

Theo grabbed a handful of tissue from the toilet roll dispenser. His mouth found Hunter's as he worked them both toward their climax, his movements unrelenting.

He swallowed Hunter's grunts of pleasure when they both came violently a moment later, his fingers closing on the heads of their pulsing shafts, capturing their shooting cum in the thick wad of tissue.

Hunter's heart raced as he continued rolling his hips helplessly against Theo's, his orgasm causing sweat to bead across his upper lip.

Theo licked at the salty drops, his hazel gaze torrid with lust as his dick throbbed and jumped against Hunter's.

Their bodies finally shuddered and stilled. Blood thundered in Hunter's head as he blinked dazedly at Theo, dumbfounded by how much pleasure he'd found in the man's arms.

Theo leaned his hot forehead against Hunter's, his breaths coming hard and fast in the aftermath of his own powerful orgasm.

"I want to fuck you so badly right now."

Hunter froze at his words.

"I—we can't," he stammered after a shocked pause.

Theo's expression grew serious. "I know. I heard what you said to those guys."

Awkward silence fell between them as they stared at one another.

"I'm sorry." Hunter pushed Theo away, zipped himself up hastily, and barged out of the cubicle.

He heard Theo call his name and practically ran out of the restrooms, scared by the feelings twisting through him. Because, for one disconcerting moment, he'd actually entertained the idea of letting Theo do exactly as he'd wanted.

CHAPTER 3

"We have an emergency," Imogen Hart declared in the tone of one announcing the end of the world and the demise of the human race as everyone knew it.

Hunter swallowed a bite of his bagel, took a sip of his coffee, and looked up leisurely from the checklists he was reviewing.

"And what, pray tell, is the emergency?" He eyed his store manager with a raised eyebrow. "Are we out of toilet rolls? Is the red light blinking on the coffee machine in the kitchen? Or did your boyfriend do something stupid again?"

This earned him a sharp look.

Hunter shrugged. "I mean, those *were* the last three major emergencies you declared this past two weeks."

Imogen narrowed her eyes at him from where she sat working at her computer. "There are days when I wonder why I bother working for you."

Hunter put his cup down and started counting on the fingers of one hand. "Because I pay you well, give you incredible staff benefits, including health insurance, and, oh, you get free access to all the rock climbing gear you want?"

Imogen muttered something rude under her breath.

It was Monday morning and they were going through the weekly inventory before they opened up for the day. Pride coursed through Hunter as he looked through the open doorway of their back office into the store.

Go Thomson! was one the most successful sports shops this side of the San Bernardino Mountains, so much so it regularly saw foot traffic from the neighboring towns.

When Hunter first told his father what his intentions were after completing college, his old man had given him a long hard look before relinquishing a tiny section of his hardware store to Hunter. Within two years, Hunter's business had expanded enough for him to purchase real estate in a prime location in town. Not only did *Go Thomson!* cater to the sports enthusiasts who lived in and around Twilight Falls, it also met the needs of the thousands of tourists who visited the San Bernardino mountains every year to indulge in their favorite outdoor activities. His idea to focus on the apparel side of the business early on had proven to be a huge hit and a steady earner during the quieter winter months. Not having any major direct competitors in and around Twilight Falls to contend with had also helped his business thrive.

"The reason I'm declaring an emergency is because I finally know the name of the company who bought the storefront opposite ours," Imogen said, her fingers moving on the mouse of her computer.

Hunter's ears perked up.

The retail premises across the road from *Go Thomson!* had been empty ever since the couple who owned the bookstore and stationary shop that once stood there retired and moved to Dallas to be closer to their son and his family eighteen months ago. The "Under Contract" sign had appeared almost as swiftly as the realtor's "For Sale" board when the property went on the market in early summer.

Despite quizzing the estate agent and his own contacts at the town administration offices, no one had been able to tell Hunter the name of the business who'd purchased the store. He rose from his desk and crossed the office to peer over Imogen's shoulder.

"So, who is it?"

"It's *Miller,* a clothing store in L.A."

Hunter frowned as he studied the slick website Imogen was scrolling through.

"They've got a shop in Malibu and Long Beach too," she murmured. "Looks like those were pretty successful business expansions from their reviews."

"What kind of clothes do they sell?"

"Hmm. Dress clothes and casual wear mostly. Says here the owner of the company likes to work with new designers fresh out of college. And he uses ethically sourced materials in all his products."

Hunter started to relax. "So, it's a fashion boutique?"

Imogen rolled her eyes at his condescending tone.

"I get that you don't usually bother with anything except for T-shirts and jeans, but other people like to dress nice." She paused. "Do you even own a tie?"

"I do."

"Let me guess. It's the one from your high school graduation."

Hunter gave her an affronted look. "College, actually. And I have a second tie. It goes with my Armani suit."

Imogen smiled wryly. "You mean the one Alex forced you to buy for his and Finn's second wedding?"

"The very same." Hunter pulled a face. "But Carter wants me to get something new for his and Elijah's wedding."

"Oh, yeah. How are their wedding plans coming along?"

"They're not. Carter's busy with his new movie project, which means the rest of us are having to babysit Maisie on some of the days when he's back in town."

Imogen stared at him, nonplussed.

Hunter grinned. "Apparently, Elijah's a bit of a screamer in the—"

"Okay, okay, I get it!" Imogen said, flushing. "Christ, I can't believe we're talking about the sex life of one of Hollywood's biggest movie stars right—"

Hunter opened his mouth.

Imogen's expression grew cool. "You're about to make a play on the word big and tell me something inane about the size of Carter Wilson's penis, aren't you?"

Hunter sucked in air and clapped his hands slowly. "Oh wow. It's like you can read my mind."

"The fact that you said that with so much pride worries me. Anyway, I found this statement on the website of *Miller*."

She clicked on the news section of the store's web page.

Hunter scanned the short article at the top. His amusement faded when he read the last paragraph.

"Oh shit."

Imogen grimaced. "Now you get why I said it was an emergency?"

Hunter straightened, his brow furrowing into an almighty scowl.

"They're gonna open a sports apparel store. Across from *mine*?!"

A young man carrying a pile of shoe boxes popped his head around the door.

"Why is Hunter shouting?" Benji Wilson asked Imogen.

Hunter glanced irately at their shop assistant before leaning past Imogen and grabbing her computer mouse.

"Your lord and master is incensed because a competitor is daring to open up shop across from us," Imogen said drily. "And the article says that only a section of the new store will be dedicated to sports apparel, so don't get your boxers in a twist."

"Well, he or she may choose to grow that side of their business once they see how successful *Go Thomson!* is," Hunter muttered, still vexed.

"What exactly are you looking for?" Imogen asked. "And please stop abusing my mouse like that. You're gonna break it."

Benji snickered.

Imogen sighed at the shop assistant. "Can you please wipe that dirty smile off your face? I am well aware that you're still under the influence of your teenage hormones, but we all know Hunter prefers playing with men's private parts as opposed to women's. If anyone should be worrying about their mouse here, it's you."

"I'm not his type," Benji stated blithely.

"He's not my type," Hunter muttered, his gaze on the computer screen. "And he's a brat." He opened up another tab and started typing.

"See? I'm a brat," Benji said with a smug smirk before disappearing in the direction of the storeroom at the back of the shop.

"Do you even have a type?" Imogen asked Hunter. "You've hardly dated in the five years I've known you. I thought you were meant to be this town's hottest bad boy."

Hunter's fingers paused above the keyboard.

A face flashed before him.

Dark hair. Hazel eyes. Sculptured cheekbones fit for a Greek god. A body to match.

"I have a type," Hunter muttered defensively, fingers flying over the keyboard once more. His expression brightened when he finally found what he was looking for. "Ah-ha! Looks like *Miller* is registered to a—"

He faltered as he stared at the name on the screen.

"A what?" Imogen peered curiously at the computer. "Oh. So, it's a guy. Theo Considine."

Hunter's heart slammed against his ribs.

It's just a coincidence. There's no way it's that *Theo!*

Guilt danced through Hunter as he thought back to that night in L.A., one month ago. After fleeing the club's restrooms and the arresting man he'd left there, he'd gone to find Tristan to tell him he was going back to the hotel. Though Hunter had done his best not to alarm his best friend, Tristan had insisted on accompanying him, despite his client's protests. After Hunter assured Tristan that he was really okay, they'd shared their cab ride in silence, Tristan too courteous to probe him about why he'd wanted to leave the club so suddenly.

Of the people close to him, only Tristan and Hunter's father knew the reason why Hunter always insisted on being a top in every relationship he had ever been in. Unfortunately, most of the men he'd been attracted to over the years had been tops too.

That night in L.A. was the first time in over ten years Hunter had contemplated submitting his body to the control of another man again. And it had scared him like little else could.

A shout reached them from the front end of the store.

"Hey guys? You gotta come see this!"

Hunter and Imogen exchanged a puzzled glance. They trooped out of the office and were joined by Benji.

Chloe Rodriguez, their second shop assistant, was standing at one of the shop's windows and staring outside.

Two large trucks emblazoned with the logo and name of the company Hunter and Imogen had just been checking out had pulled up across the road. The drivers jumped out and eyed the empty store opposite *Go Thomson!*

"Oh," Benji mumbled. "I know that shop. My cousin in Long Beach can't stop raving about their clothes."

The rumble of an expensive engine echoed down the road. A black Jaguar coupe with red rims slowed and parked neatly behind the second truck. Hunter's stomach lurched when he saw the smartly-dressed man who stepped out of the sleek sports car.

Dark hair. Hazel eyes. Sculptured cheekbones fit for a Greek god. A body to match.

It *was* Theo from the nightclub in L.A.

CHAPTER 4

THEO PUT DOWN THE BOX HE WAS CARRYING, WINCED, AND rubbed the back of his neck.

"You okay, boss?"

Theo turned.

A young man with specs and an anxious expression was peering at him through the doorway of the back office.

"Yeah." Theo grimaced. "I think I pulled something in my neck last night. I'm still not used to the pillow in my hotel."

Codie Symonds, the freshly appointed manager of the *Miller* store in Twilight Falls, bobbed his chin nervously.

"You're moving into a place in that gated estate on the edge of town, right? It's really nice out there."

Theo smiled. "I've heard it is. And Codie?"

"Yeah?"

"Call me Theo."

Codie opened his mouth, hesitated, and nodded shyly.

Theo watched the young man head out into the busy

store where his L.A. display designer and business partner Kate Vincent and the rest of the local staff were busy unpacking the last of their stock. Even though Codie had been in retail for five years since he'd left college, it was his first gig as a store manager.

Kate had had some doubts about whether the young man was the right person for the job when she and Theo had interviewed candidates for the job a month ago. Theo had reassured her that he was the perfect guy for the position. Codie's resume and references spoke for themselves; as for his timid manner, Theo suspected that would disappear once he took command of the store.

He smiled faintly as he started unpacking the contents of the box.

Besides, I have yet to be wrong about any of the decisions I've made when it comes to my company.

It had been three days since he'd moved to Twilight Falls to supervise the opening of the latest branch of *Miller*. Just as he'd done for their Malibu and Long Beach offshoots, Theo intended to be around for the first two months of their new business venture, while Kate held the fort at their L.A. base.

Commuting to Malibu and Long Beach from his home in L.A. hadn't been a problem. Twilight Falls was a different matter. Theo didn't fancy spending long hours on the interstate and had elected to rent a place locally instead.

As far as Theo was concerned, this was the most critical phase of any enterprise and would determine a store's success or failure.

It was Kate who'd spied the empty business locale in a

prime location in the picturesque town on a weekend trip with her boyfriend. They had been scouting the area around L.A. for a possible new store for several months and had yet to come up with a promising venue.

Twilight Falls hadn't even been on Theo's radar. But a couple of visits to the place soon changed his mind. With the amount of foot traffic the town saw from the neighboring communities and the dedication of its mayor and council to facilitate the lives of small business owners operating there, the place had oodles of potential for *Miller*.

Just as he and Kate had done for their Malibu and Long Beach branches, they'd decide to focus a section of the store on the specific needs of the local townsfolk. In the case of Twilight Falls, sports apparel and winter clothes had been the obvious choices.

Their only major competitor was opposite the road from them.

From the information Kate had gathered from their local staff, *Go Thomson!* had been in business for a while and was going from strength to strength every year. They specialized in sports gear and apparel and were well known outside the area.

Theo finished setting up his stuff around the office he would be sharing with Codie and decided it was time to head across the way and say hello to his neighbor and competitor before grabbing lunch for his staff.

The bell above the entrance of *Go Thomson!* jangled when he opened it a moment later. Theo stepped inside the warm, airy space and looked around curiously. It only took a few seconds for him to figure out why the business was so successful.

Whoever is in charge of their stock and display design is good.

He glanced from the two shop assistants who were helping out customers, to the petite woman with the shock of strawberry hair behind the sales counter. Her eyes twinkled warmly as she looked up.

"Welcome to *Go Thomson!* How can I help—Oh." She paused, her expression growing stilted. "Er, hello."

Ah. She knows who I am.

Theo gave her his most dazzling smile.

"Hey. I'm Theo Miller, the owner of *Miller*. Nice to meet you."

HUNTER IGNORED THE DISTANT SOUND OF THE BELL AND the murmur of voices coming from the shop.

He was analyzing the sales figures of *Go Thomson!* for the last quarter and making notes as to where he should concentrate his efforts if his new rival proved to be a problem for his business. A frown furrowed his brow as he stared at the same column of numbers for the third time in as many minutes.

Focus, damnit.

The numbers blurred and were replaced by series of vivid images.

Green-tinted hazel eyes dilated with passion. A sexy mouth opened on throaty grunts of pleasure. Lips and a tongue that had scorched Hunter's senses and melted his thoughts until his brain was a puddle of rose-tinted goo. A large hand cupping and rubbing Hunter's straining erection with a masterful touch.

Hunter's dick throbbed as he recollected every single, graphic moment of the minutes he had spent with Theo in that restroom in L.A. for what felt like the hundredth time since the man reappeared in his life three days ago.

Of all the places he could have chosen to open a new store, why the hell did it have to be Twilight Falls?

Hunter scowled. He didn't intend to find out the answer to that question. Just as he had no intention of meeting the man. As far as he was concerned, he was going to do his damndest to avoid the guy who'd occupied his thoughts on and off for the last month.

Imogen stuck her head around the door. "You have a visitor."

Hunter stared. Imogen had the strangest expression on her face.

A figure appeared behind her.

The object of Hunter's fantasies walked into his office.

"Hello. I thought it was about time I introduced—"

The man froze in his tracks. His hazel eyes widened.

Hunter swallowed.

So much for avoiding him.

CHAPTER 5

THEO STARED UNBLINKINGLY AT THE MAN SITTING motionless behind the desk.

"Hunter, this is Theo Miller, the owner of *Miller*. Theo, this is Hunter Thomson, my boss." The redhead, whose name was Imogen, smiled politely at Theo. "Would you like a coffee?"

"Yes. That would be—"

"No!"

They both turned and stared at the man who had jumped to his feet and was glaring at them from the other side of the room.

Imogen flashed Theo an apologetic glance before frowning at Hunter.

"Hmm, Hunter, you're being a bit—"

"It's okay," Theo murmured. "Hunter and I…know each other."

Imogen's eyes rounded. "You do?"

Her gaze shifted to Hunter, her expression indicating that her boss was in for a serious grilling later.

Guilt clashed with irritation in Hunter's eyes.

"I'm sorry. A coffee would be great."

Tense silence fell between them after Imogen exited the office.

"I thought your name was Considine," Hunter said gruffly.

"Considine is my mother's maiden name."

Theo looked around the room, giving Hunter the space he so obviously needed. His own pulse was still racing from the shock of meeting the man who had plagued his fantasies for the better part of the last month.

To think I'd finally find my mystery guy here.

Their torrid encounter in L.A. was still very much at the forefront of Theo's mind. It had been some time since he'd experienced the sizzling sexual chemistry he'd felt with Hunter that night. In fact, if Theo was being completely honest with himself, it was the first time he'd been that insanely attracted to someone at their very first meeting.

Theo was by no means a saint when it came to sex. He'd started liking guys when he was in middle school. After going out with a couple of girls in high school and discovering that, though he liked them, they didn't turn him on, he finally came out as gay. It wasn't until college that he entered into his first serious relationship with a man. The affair didn't last long and they parted ways amicably, Theo going on to have a series of short-lived flings in the years that followed.

He'd realized by then that he was far from ready to settle into a serious relationship and decided to concentrate his energy on growing his business instead.

Hunter was the first man Theo hadn't been able to stop thinking about. Though they hadn't had penetrative sex, Theo couldn't remember the last time a guy had excited him so much or made him come so hard he'd seen stars. But by the time he'd followed Hunter out of the restrooms and into the club that night, his gray-eyed Lothario had pulled a disappearing act.

Having resigned himself to likely never crossing paths with the man who'd become a steady fixture in his sexual fantasies in the past few weeks, Theo was stunned to find him in the last place he'd ever expected to.

Hunter's office was cozier than his own room in the store across the road. Pictures depicting Twilight Falls and its surrounding valley and mountains under all four seasons crowded two of the walls. There were a lot of personal photographs too, most of them showing Hunter among a group of laughing men or engaged in a variety of outdoor activities.

Theo's curiosity roused when he saw a cluster of black and white photos next to the window. He walked over and examined them closely.

"You climb?"

"Yeah, I do," Hunter murmured reluctantly.

Theo turned to face him.

The gray eyes observing him were still full of suspicion.

Theo bit back a smile.

He's like a cat.

"So do I," he drawled.

Hunter blinked at that. "You do?"

Theo chuckled softly. "You don't have to look so shocked."

Imogen appeared with their coffee.

"Yell if you need anything," she said as she headed back into the store, her curious gaze lingering on them.

"Christ, I'm never gonna hear the end of this," Hunter muttered after she'd gone.

Theo leaned a hip against the window sill. "Does she know you're gay?"

"The whole town knows I'm gay," Hunter grunted.

"Oh," Theo murmured. "Then, are you seeing anyone?"

Hunter eyed him warily as he brought his cup to his lips.

"Not that it's any of your business, but no, I'm not."

"So, why did you run?" Theo said quietly.

Hunter choked on his drink.

"Sorry." Theo crossed the floor and thumped Hunter firmly on the back while he coughed.

Hunter grabbed a tissue from a dispenser on his desk and dabbed at the coffee he'd spewed onto his T-shirt and chin. He glared at Theo.

"Are you always this forward?"

Theo shrugged. "Yeah." He paused while Hunter discarded the soiled tissue. "I went looking for you, that night in L.A."

Hunter stiffened, his expression growing guarded once more.

"Why?"

"Because I liked the way you felt in my arms."

Hunter's eyes flared at Theo's calm confession. The way he frowned while his cheeks bloomed with color made Theo want to take him in his arms again and kiss him senseless.

Yup. A cute, prickly cat.

"Jesus, I can't believe you said that with a straight face," Hunter mumbled.

"I don't like playing games."

Hunter raked a hand through his hair, clearly ruffled by their candid conversation.

"Look, you need to back up a bit."

Theo's pulse accelerated at what he read in the stormy gray gaze opposite him.

So, he's as aware of me as I am of him.

He took a deliberate step toward Hunter and leaned in close.

"Why, am I crowding you in?" he said huskily.

Hunter swallowed convulsively and started to move back. He scowled in the next instant and stayed put.

Theo smiled. "I like that about you."

"Like what?" Hunter's eyelashes swept down as his gaze dropped to Theo's mouth.

Theo's dick throbbed with a wave of arousal.

He could see the pulse beating frantically at the base of Hunter's throat. He bit back a groan when he recalled how good Hunter's skin had tasted when he'd kissed him there.

"That you're ballsy. And that you can't hide that you like me too."

Hunter's gaze shot up at that. "Who said I like—"

Theo finally gave in to temptation and took the mouth of the sexy man sassing him.

Hunter gasped.

He did not step back. Nor did he break contact.

They stared breathlessly at one another as Theo slowly and tentatively explored Hunter's lips.

This wasn't like their first kiss, which had been hot and fast and hungry.

Instead, this was a leisurely mission of discovery.

Theo's hands found Hunter's waist. He clasped him gently and pulled him close. Hunter didn't resist. Instead, he shuddered and closed his eyes as Theo brushed and caressed and sucked lightly on his lips, his arms rising languidly to lock around Theo's nape.

Theo groaned at the way Hunter was melting against him. He probed Hunter's lips and was rewarded with a sultry little sound as Hunter opened his mouth and let him in.

"Sorry to disturb you guys, but I have a—*Oh crap, sorry!*"

Hunter froze in Theo's arms. His eyes slammed open, horror draining some of the color from his face.

Theo sighed and reluctantly let go of the man whose mouth he was ravishing, his arms feeling strangely bereft as he lowered them to his sides.

They both turned and looked guiltily at the red-faced woman standing frozen in the doorway of the office, the paperwork she'd been holding in her hands fluttering to the ground from her limp fingers.

Imogen recovered her senses, stooped, and gathered the documents hastily.

"I'll, er, be out in the shop!" she squealed before bolting out of the room.

"Shit," Hunter muttered.

CHAPTER 6

"SPILL," IMOGEN DEMANDED.

Hunter eyed her uneasily over the ribs and potato salad the waitress had just delivered to their table. Imogen had dragged him out for an early dinner and was studying him like an executioner would his prisoner where they sat next to a bay window in their favorite family restaurant.

"I'd rather not."

She ignored his rebuttal. "Where and how did you and Theo meet?"

Hunter wordlessly tucked into his food.

Imogen narrowed her eyes at his mutinous silence.

"Maybe I should ask Theo."

Alarm shot through Hunter.

"If you do that, I won't give you any of the new climbing gear coming in next week," he threatened.

Imogen's expression fell. "Man, that's mean."

"What's mean?"

Hunter stiffened. He looked over his shoulder.

Great. Just what I need right now.

Tristan was standing behind him with Alex Hancock-West and Wyatt Batista. Along with Carter Wilson, Drake Jackson, and Miles Martinez, they made up the Terrible Seven, a group of close friends who'd grown up together in Twilight Falls and gone on to cause havoc for their teachers, parents, and local law enforcers throughout their school years.

"We saw you from outside," Tristan said lightly. "Mind if we join you?"

Imogen's face glazed over. She'd been a fan of the Terrible Seven since forever and loved nothing more than ogling them close-up.

"Please do," she gushed, pulling a free chair over.

Hunter cut his eyes to her. She smiled blithely at his warning expression.

It wasn't until they'd sat down and ordered drinks and food that Tristan looked curiously from Hunter to Imogen and back again. He'd evidently detected the underlying current of tension running between them.

"What's the matter?"

"Nothing," Hunter said sharply.

Imogen carefully stabbed a chunk of potato. He could tell she was dying to spill the beans on what she'd witnessed at lunchtime that day.

"Anyone else seen that new place opening up opposite Hunter's yet?" Alex asked. "I've been to their L.A. shop. They've got a really nice clothing range."

Frozen silence fell across the table.

Alex and Wyatt finally picked up on the awkward mood and gave Hunter and Imogen puzzled looks.

Tristan frowned. "Seriously, what's wrong?"

"Stuff the climbing gear," Imogen told Hunter militantly. "This is too good not to share!" She leaned across the table and beckoned Tristan, Alex, and Wyatt closer. "So, that new store is owned by this really hot guy called Theo Miller," she hissed in a conspiratorial tone. "He came to our shop today. He and Hunter know each other. And you're never going to guess what happened—"

"Fine!" Hunter snapped. He threw his napkin down on the table and grabbed his beer. "Theo and I met a month ago, in L.A. We hooked up for one night. There, end of story." He swallowed a large gulp of his drink.

Imogen's eyes rounded. "Whaaat?! I never heard anything about this!"

"Contrary to popular belief, there is no law that says I have to report every aspect of my personal life to you," Hunter retorted.

Tristan stared. "Wait. A month ago? Do you mean at that club?" Lines wrinkled his brow. "Was this guy the reason why you were so upset?"

"What?" Alex said, startled. Wyatt looked similarly surprised.

"Why, did something bad happen?" Imogen mumbled, her expression turning anxious.

"Nothing bad happened," Hunter protested. "We jerked each other off and that was that."

"Oh." Relief washed across Imogen's face. She grimaced. "Okay, now that that graphic image has been burned into my retina, the two of you kissed today. And you both looked like you were enjoying it." She paused. "It didn't feel like the end of anything to me."

Hunter's ears warmed. He could hardly deny this.

Theo's slow, measured kiss has been as addictive as the feverish ones they'd shared in the club in L.A. a month ago.

It was all he'd been able to think about that afternoon. Not that he was going to admit this to Imogen or his friends.

Tristan's frown deepened. "He kissed you?"

Guilt twisted through Hunter at his best friend's irate look.

"It's okay. It's not like he forced himself on me."

Alex and Wyatt glanced between the two of them, now totally bewildered.

"Nothing's gonna come of it," Hunter stated, his voice hardening. "He's not my type and I have no interest in pursuing any kind of relationship with him."

Imogen looked doubtful at that.

The waitress came over with the rest of their order, putting a stop to their conversation.

"Anyway, aren't we meant to play poker this Saturday?" Hunter said after they all tucked into their food. "How come you guys are out tonight?"

"These two needed to drown their sorrows," Tristan said, indicating Alex and Wyatt.

Hunter stared quizzically at the two men.

A troubled expression washed across Alex and Wyatt's faces.

"I had a fall out with Finn," Alex mumbled.

"I think Nathan knows how I feel about him," Wyatt confessed.

Hunter's eyes widened. "Nathan? As in your business partner in the design firm? *That* Nathan?!"

Tristan raised an eyebrow. "Oh. You didn't know?"

"No!" Hunter blurted.

"Your powers of observation are terrible, as always," Alex said wryly.

"Wow." Imogen grabbed a French fry and stared at Wyatt. "A friend of a friend of mine went on a few dates with Nathan. Apparently, that guy is some kind of god in the sack. So, he's your type, huh?"

Wyatt looked like he wanted to sink into the ground. "It's not like I planned to fall for him. It kinda just happened."

Hunter decided to give him some breathing space and switched his attention to Alex. "What's this about a fall out with Finn?"

"They didn't actually have a falling out." Tristan rolled his eyes. "He's pouting because Finn is ignoring him."

"I'm not pouting," Alex protested, a trace of guilt underscoring his voice. "It's just that Finn gets, well—he gets pretty single-minded when he's in the middle of a project, to the point he barely eats and sleeps. He started working on a new commission a week ago and I've barely seen him."

"So what you're really saying is that you're not getting enough sex," Hunter stated leadenly.

Tristan hid a smile behind his beer. Wyatt heaved a heavy sigh.

Alex glowered at Hunter. "I'm not saying any such thing."

"Yeah, you are," Imogen said.

"If you want sex, why don't you seduce him?" Hunter said.

"I—" Alex stopped. "I suppose I could," he mumbled, looking visibly deflated.

Hunter stabbed a rib with his fork and pointed it at Alex. "Or are you saying the honeymoon is over and your insanely hot husband is no longer interested in you?"

Alex narrowed his eyes. "Trust me, he's interested."

"Well, there you go then." Hunter turned to Wyatt. "So, Nathan is definitely straight?"

"Yeah," Wyatt murmured. "One hundred percent."

"Why do you think he knows how you feel about him?"

Wyatt mumbled something indistinct.

"What?" Hunter said.

"I kissed him," Wyatt said in a miserable voice. "He came over one night. We had too much to drink. He fell asleep on the couch and I—" he paused and raked a hand through his hair, "well, I gave in to temptation and kissed him."

Tristan grimaced. "He woke up?"

"Yeah."

"Dude," Alex muttered.

"He claims he doesn't remember much about what happened that night, but things have been awkward between us since," Wyatt admitted.

"What are you going to do?" Hunter said after a short silence.

Wyatt shrugged. "Nothing. I don't want to jeopardize our business relationship, so I'll just have to keep these feelings to myself."

Hunter was still mulling over Wyatt's words when he drove into his estate an hour later. Of all of the Terrible

Seven, Wyatt was the quietest and the one with the biggest heart. If anyone deserved to be happy, it was him.

Lights were on in the house opposite his when he turned into the cul-de-sac where he lived. He pulled into his drive, his gaze on the property across the road.

The place was a rental and had been unoccupied for over a year.

Hunter frowned. *The realtor must have leased it again.*

He stepped out of his Jeep and was about to close the door when he spied the silhouette of a car on the sloping driveway opposite his. He stared.

It was a black Jaguar coupe with red rims.

Hunter's stomach flip-flopped. The license plate looked familiar. As did the car.

No way.

The front door of the house opened. A man came out, strolled down the porch steps, and headed for the vehicle. He stopped when he saw Hunter standing frozen on his driveway. The man turned. Surprise flared on his face. An amused smile curved his mouth an instant later.

"Hey there, neighbor," Theo greeted with a small wave.

"No fucking way," Hunter mumbled.

CHAPTER 7

"It's like it was meant to be," Imogen declared. "He bought the store opposite yours. Now he's renting the place across from you. Yup, I can feel the hands of fate at work."

Hunter frowned as he finished rearranging the window display they were putting together. "It's just a coincidence."

Imogen made a face and squatted back on her heels. "Coincidence my butt. Just admit that you like the guy already."

"I'll admit no such thing," Hunter protested.

He found himself glancing across the road despite himself.

A large banner dominated the store front above *Miller*.

Theo's store was opening in less than a week. From the flurry of activity Hunter had witnessed this week, team *Miller* was in countdown mode for the big day.

The front door of the store opened just as Hunter rose to his feet. Theo stepped out and turned to talk to someone inside the shop. He paused on the sidewalk and smiled when he saw Hunter and Imogen in the window of *Go Thomson!* He gave them a friendly wave before strolling up the road.

"Oh wow," Imogen muttered. "Your tongue is practically hanging out of your mouth."

"It is not." Hunter ignored the butterflies in his stomach and dragged his gaze from Theo's back.

Just because the man looks gorgeous in every damn thing he wears doesn't mean I'm attracted to him.

His libido disagreed strongly with this internal statement.

It was Chloe who alerted them to the radio interview an hour later.

"Hey, you guys?" She popped her head around the door of the office and waved her phone at them. "I think that Miller person is live on the air."

Hunter and Imogen stared at one another before jumping from their chairs and crowding around the shop assistant.

The popular pop song that had been playing ended and the local radio DJ came on.

"Hi there, Twilight Falls, it's your favorite DJ, Jerry Ball here. Boy do we have a surprise for you today. In the studio with me right now is Theo Miller, the owner of the fabulous new clothing store opening in Twilight Falls this Monday. Theo, it's great to have you here. And can I just say? I wish our listeners could see you right now. You look absolutely divine! Is that *Miller* stock you're wearing?"

The DJ's flirtatious tone sent a sharp pang twisting

through Hunter's gut. He stiffened at the unwelcome sensation.

"Christ, I think Gary's in love again," Imogen muttered.

Chloe grinned. The DJ had a habit of falling for someone new each month. It seemed Theo would be the subject of his affections this time around.

The voice that had haunted Hunter's dreams for the last week rumbled through the phone speakers and sent a shiver of desire down his spine.

"Hi, Jerry," Theo drawled. "It's great to be here. And thank you for the compliment. Yes, this ensemble is from the current *Miller* line. Our products are pretty bespoke and we have some incredibly talented designers working for us, so I'm proud to say my wardrobe is full of *Miller* stock."

"Ho boy," Chloe started fanning herself while the DJ continued questioning his guest in syrupy tones. "Is it me, or does this Theo guy sound like he's stripping you with every syllable he utters?"

"It's not just you." Imogen ignored Hunter's irritated expression. "I bet half the women in Twilight Falls turn up for the opening of *Miller* just to get an eyeful of the owner." She gave Hunter a jaundiced look. "How the hell you can resist this guy is beyond me. If I wasn't a taken woman, I'd be all over him like white on rice."

"Well, you're welcome to him," Hunter grumbled.

Chloe stared. "Wait? You two have a thing going on?!"

"They kissed when Theo came to our store," Imogen said.

A gasp sounded behind them.

"They did not?!" Benji clutched his chest and gaped from where he'd joined them after serving their last customer.

"It was a one-time thing," Hunter said defensively.

"Yeah, right," Imogen muttered.

Chloe sucked in air at her expression.

"You mean—there was more than *kissing?!"* she squealed.

Benji gave Hunter an awed stare. "Dude."

Imogen hushed them.

It was at the end of the interview that Theo dropped the bombshell that would make Hunter incensed for the rest of that day.

"Before you go, I hear there's something special in store for the opening day of *Miller* next week," the DJ said. "Can you let us in on the secret?"

"Sure," Theo replied. "I believe you have your very own Hollywood star living here in Twilight Falls. He kindly agreed to model our latest clothing range next Monday. I couldn't be more pleased to have Carter Wilson showcase the *Miller* brand to the people of Twilight Falls."

Hunter swore.

CARTER MET HUNTER'S IRATE GLARE WITH A SHRUG. "What?"

"Don't 'what' me, you traitor!" Hunter hissed.

They were in the kitchen of *La Petite Bouche Gourmande,* the bakery of Elijah Davis, Carter's fiancé. Hunter had come over to commiserate with Elijah and discovered Carter hiding from his horde of fans who normally haunted the shop.

Elijah looked up from where he and Maisie were icing a cake.

"What's wrong?"

"Your fiancé here is helping my enemy," Hunter grumbled.

Elijah brightened. "Oh, you mean that new store opening up across from you? I hear their clothes are nice."

Hunter groaned. "Your fathers are terrible friends, Maisie."

Carter's niece came over and took Hunter's hand. "Has Papa Carter upset you?" she said solemnly. "Do you want me to tell him off?"

Hunter sighed and dropped a kiss on the little girl's hair. "It's okay, sweetie. I'll come up with a plan to punish your papa later."

Carter sighed. "Theo is a friend of a friend of mine. And I owe that guy a favor for keeping the paparazzi off my tail when I took Elijah and Maisie to Paris last month. Besides, I'm only going to be at Theo's store a couple of hours, max."

"How come you've never modeled for *Go Thomson!*?" Hunter said grouchily.

Carter narrowed his eyes. "Because you never asked."

Hunter was still in a foul mood when he headed over to *The Watering Hole* for a drink later that night. Though he normally didn't visit the gay bar during the week, he felt the need to unwind before he went home. He was debating whether to invite Tristan over when he saw

Drake Jackson at the bar. He made his way through the crowd, climbed onto the empty bar stool next to the builder, and ordered a beer.

"You've been glaring at that bottle for a good five minutes now," Drake drawled after a while. "At this rate, neither of us is gonna hook up with anyone tonight. What's eating you?"

"I have business trouble brewing," Hunter mumbled.

Drake raised an eyebrow. "What kind of business trouble?"

Hunter told him briefly about Theo and the *Miller* store.

"Sounds to me like your problem is more with this guy rather than the fact that he's your business rival."

"Why does everyone seem to think that there's something going on between me and Theo?" Hunter groaned.

Drake smiled faintly. "Maybe because you make it so obvious there is?"

A sudden bark of laughter distracted them.

Hunter looked around and froze.

Theo stood amidst a small group of men at the end of the bar. He was dressed in jeans, a white T-shirt, a corduroy jacket, and brown brogues. As usual, he seemed oblivious to the avid stares he was drawing.

One of the men he was with, a guy with bleached blond hair and an inebriated expression, put his hand on Theo's chest and gazed at him as if he was a piece of prime beef steak.

Hunter's knuckles whitened on his beer.

"Isn't that our local gay DJ?" Drake murmured.

CHAPTER 8

I REALLY SHOULDN'T HAVE ACCEPTED HIS INVITATION.

Theo kept a polite smile on his face as he engaged in light conversation with Jerry. It was obvious the guy was trying to hit on him.

Unfortunately, the only man I'm interested in right now is the one who owns the store across the road from me.

"Who wants another round of drinks?" the DJ asked in a slurred voice.

"I think you might have had enough," one of his friends said, sending an apologetic glance Theo's way. "Why don't I get you some water?"

"I'll go," Theo said, relieved at the chance to be able to escape. He headed through the packed bar before any of them could stop him.

A familiar headful of hair caught his gaze a moment later. Theo's pulse spiked as he studied the figure moving through the crowd to his right.

"Hunter?"

Hunter froze. He turned around slowly.

"Hey," he muttered, not quite meeting Theo's eyes.

Theo masked a puzzled frown at his shuttered expression. He looked at the tall man with dark hair and blue eyes next to Hunter.

"Hi, I'm Theo."

"Drake." The guy shook his hand and glanced over his shoulder. "Looks like your friend is looking for you."

Theo followed his gaze to where the DJ was waving at him. "He's not really my friend." He grimaced slightly. "To be honest, I was regretting having agreed to come here tonight." He turned and gazed warmly at Hunter. "I'm glad I did now."

A mutinous light flashed in Hunter's eyes at that.

"Really? Well, I'm not," he snapped. "Goodnight."

Hunter grabbed Drake's arm and dragged him toward the far side of the room.

"Hey, that was uncalled for," Drake murmured.

Theo stared after them, surprised.

He's definitely unhappy about something.

It wasn't until he came out to the restrooms of *The Watering Hole* half an hour later and found Hunter waiting for him in the corridor that Theo finally got the chance to find out exactly what was bugging the man who'd been on his mind for the past week.

"We need to talk," Hunter said in a hard voice.

Theo couldn't help but suppress a smile despite the awkwardness of the situation. Hunter all serious was a real turn on.

In fact, everything this guy does turns me on.

"I thought you were avoiding me," Theo said lightly.

Hunter narrowed his eyes. "I was. But, considering we

work and live across from one another, we can't exactly stay out of each other's way. I want to make some things clear."

Yeah, he definitely has his guard up.

Theo spied a door at the end of the corridor. "Want to take this outside?"

Hunter hesitated. "Sure."

Theo led the way, curious as to what it was that had Hunter so disgruntled.

They came out onto a terrace with an outdoor seating area that spilled over into a pleasant summer garden. Theo leaned a shoulder against a post, stuffed his hands into the pockets of his jeans, and crossed his ankles.

"So, what do you want to talk about?" he murmured, leveling a curious look at Hunter.

Hunter stayed a few feet away, his posture strangely defensive.

"I don't appreciate you using my friends for your business," he said brusquely.

Surprise darted through Theo.

Now this I was not expecting.

"I'm not quite sure what you mean."

"I'm talking about Carter." A muscle jumped in Hunter's jawline.

Theo watched Hunter for a moment, unsure what it was he was reading in his tense face.

"I didn't know Carter was your friend until you told me just now," he said quietly. "I approached him after a mutual acquaintance told me he lived locally." He paused. "I would have thought he would have rejected my offer if he'd felt there was a conflict of interest."

Hunter fisted his hands. "Well, there is! I'm gonna be one of his best men."

Understanding dawned inside Theo as he finally recognized the reason behind Hunter's militant expression. It was becoming clear to him that this wasn't about Carter modeling for the opening of *Miller*.

Hunter was telling him to stay out of his life, period.

Theo frowned slightly.

There can only be one explanation for why he's acting this way.

Theo decided to test his theory. He straightened and slowly closed the distance to Hunter.

Hunter's eyes widened. He took a step back, faltered, and stood his ground.

Theo bit back a grin.

Yeah, he's definitely trying to fight the attraction between us.

"Say I were to cancel Carter's appearance at my store next Monday," Theo drawled. "What would you offer me in exchange to make up for it?"

"Offer you?" Hunter mumbled.

Theo's heartbeat accelerated when he noted the pulse beating furiously at the base of Hunter's throat. Despite his apparent displeasure, Hunter's eyes had darkened, his pupils were dilated, and his mouth had parted slightly as he stared at Theo.

Damn, he's sexy.

"Yeah, offer me," Theo said in a low, sultry voice.

Hunter's gaze dropped to Theo's mouth.

Shit. Does he even know how he's looking at me right now?

Theo raised a hand and ran his thumb lightly across

Hunter's mouth, unable to resist touching him. Hunter inhaled shakily.

Theo swallowed a curse and lowered his head.

Hunter's hands rose to clutch Theo's shoulders as Theo took his mouth in a hard kiss, his eyelashes fluttering closed. Theo molded their lips together before delving inside Hunter's mouth and entwining his tongue with Hunter's.

A low sound escaped Hunter. His fingers dug into Theo's flesh.

The back door opened.

"There you are. I was wondering where you'd—Oh." Drake stilled on the threshold, a surprised look on his face. "Sorry."

Theo reluctantly took his mouth off Hunter's. Hunter opened his eyes and blinked dazedly at Theo.

"I'm not backing down," Theo told Hunter quietly. "From Carter modeling for my store's opening, or from what's between us."

Theo stepped past Drake and headed back inside the bar.

CHAPTER 9

"Wow," Imogen murmured. "I can't believe the line goes all the way down the road."

Hunter stared at the crowd of people outside *Miller*.

It was Monday morning and there was still ample time left until the store's grand opening. People had been queuing up outside even as Hunter turned up for work an hour ago.

"I don't think this is just because of Carter," Imogen said dubiously.

A yellow Maserati pulled up behind Theo's Jaguar a moment later. Excited shouts reached Hunter and Imogen through the frontage of *Go Thomson!* when Carter stepped out of the sports car. The movie star took his sunglasses off, acknowledged his fans with a wave and his usual charismatic smile, and went inside the store.

Hunter frowned.

He'd lost a lot of sleep over the last few days thinking about what Theo had told him at the bar. The fact that Theo had deliberately stayed out of his way since then should have come as a relief. Yet, not seeing Theo had only served to make Hunter more antsy.

He knew Theo was giving him space to mollify him and to allow him time to process what he'd said to him that night. Still, Hunter couldn't deny that he was a little disappointed.

He masked his disenchantment behind a neutral expression and turned away from the front windows of his store. "Let's check the inventory."

The day passed more swiftly than Hunter thought it would. He did his best to ignore the packed shop opposite *Go Thomson!* whenever he was serving customers and kept himself busy planning their autumn stock in the back office.

Lights were still on in *Miller* when Hunter closed his store that evening.

He headed home still feeling despondent, showered, and was having a beer on his back porch while he contemplated what to make for dinner when his doorbell rang.

Hunter frowned and checked his phone. None of his friends had messaged to say they would be dropping by. He rose, strolled through the house, and peered curiously through the front door's peephole.

Theo was standing on his porch.

Hunter's pulse accelerated. He swallowed, wiped his suddenly damp palms on his jeans, and plastered a calm expression on his face. He opened the door and was immediately engulfed by the beguiling scent of Theo's cologne.

Theo was still in his work clothes and looked as alluring as always.

Lust twisted Hunter's belly.

"Hey," Theo said with a smile, oblivious to the sudden desire swarming Hunter. "I brought drinks and your favorite takeout." He waved a bag bearing the name of Hunter's go-to Chinese restaurant in one hand and an expensive bottle of champagne in the other.

Hunter clamped down on his filthy thoughts.

His stomach rumbled at the heavenly smell wafting from the bag.

"How did you know that was my favorite takeout?" Hunter did his best to sound cold. "And what exactly are you doing here?"

Theo grinned. "A little birdie told me you like that place, so I thought I'd bring a peace offering. And I'm celebrating the successful launch of my new store." He slipped past Hunter and entered the house as if he belonged there.

Hunter turned and frowned at him. "I didn't say you could come in." He closed the door and sighed. "You should hardly be carousing with your business rival. What if I get you drunk and extract some vital information to sabotage your business?"

"You're hardly the sabotaging type," Theo stated breezily. "Now, where's your kitchen?"

Hunter groaned. "I don't think I can eat anything

else." He burped gently behind a hand, patted his stomach, and sat back in his chair.

"You sure are a healthy eater," Theo said, his expression amused.

Hunter glanced at his empty plate before narrowing his eyes at Theo.

"Is that code for 'you-just-stuffed-your-face-stupid-because-you're-a-greedy-pig'?"

Theo chuckled at his vexed tone, gathered the dirty dishes, and headed over to the sink.

"You don't have to wash up," Hunter protested as Theo rolled his shirt sleeves up.

"I insist. And I didn't say that." Theo looked him up and down. "You must have a high metabolic rate to be so fit. That, or you exercise a lot."

Hunter ignored the hot feeling that ran through him at Theo's interested stare. He climbed to his feet, crossed the kitchen, and leaned a hip against the counter next to Theo. He watched Theo broodingly above his glass of champagne.

He was feeling slightly buzzed from the alcohol and was aware things might get risky if he drank more, but he found himself not caring about the consequences, which was a shock in itself.

"I do have a higher than average metabolic rate." Hunter arched an eyebrow. "*And* I exercise a lot. What about you?" He raked Theo's body with his gaze. "How do you keep...fit?"

Theo's eyes sparkled at Hunter's insolent look.

"I run. And I swim. I also like to do," Theo's gaze

dropped briefly to Hunter's mouth, "—stuff in the bedroom."

Hunter's dick stirred at Theo's provocative words.

Theo smiled, as if he knew exactly what was going on inside Hunter's jeans.

"And I like rock climbing."

Hunter blinked. He'd forgotten about that.

"Have you been to any of the climbing spots around here?"

Theo dried his hands and turned to face Hunter. "Not yet." He lifted Hunter's glass from his grasp and took a casual sip of his champagne before returning it. "Care to show me?"

Hunter's stomach flip-flopped.

Shit.

Theo in seduction mode was downright dangerous.

Hunter cleared his throat, blood thumping rapidly in his veins.

"I'm going climbing with Imogen this weekend if you want to come."

Theo's face lit up. "That would be great." He headed over to the table, took the bottle of champagne, and topped off Hunter's glass.

"Are you trying to get me drunk?" Hunter grumbled.

Theo poured the last of the champagne into his own glass and leaned around Hunter to place the empty bottle on the counter.

Hunter swallowed at Theo's closeness.

The teasing look on Theo's face told Hunter he'd noticed his reaction. "What if I were?"

Hunter attempted his most aloof look. "I'd say it wouldn't get you anywhere."

Theo leaned in close. "Are you sure?" he whispered in Hunter's right ear.

Theo's heated breath raised goosebumps on Hunter's skin and caused his body temperature to spike. He shivered and closed his eyes, hunger swirling through his belly.

"That's cheating," he mumbled.

"All's fair in love and war," Theo drawled.

Hunter opened his eyes.

Theo was grinning at him. "Goodnight. I'll pop by your store tomorrow and get details of our weekend meet up." He kissed the tip of Hunter's nose, turned, and walked out of the house.

Hunter touched his nose and stared blankly at the spot Theo had occupied a mere moment ago, conscious of the erection pressing against the zipper of his jeans.

Wait. Did he just leave me high and dry?!

The last words Theo had uttered stayed with Hunter long after he'd gone.

CHAPTER 10

"YOU SURE ARE TAKING YOUR SWEET TIME," IMOGEN muttered, securing her harness.

Hunter finished coiling their climbing rope and gave her a haughty look. "Safety first."

Imogen made a face. "I do believe you're stalling to avoid seeing Theo. It's a gorgeous day and I'm about to indulge in my favorite activity with two of the hottest guys in town, so hurry it up."

"You make it sound as if we're about to have a threesome," Hunter said scathingly. "And complimenting your boss won't earn you a raise."

Imogen stuck her tongue out at him, grabbed the rest of their kit, and headed onto the dirt path that cut through the woods. Hunter sighed, slammed the trunk of the Jeep shut, and followed her.

It was Sunday morning and they were at their favorite climbing spot outside town. The sky was a dazzling blue and the sun sparkled off the river meandering through the valley to their left. Hunter's tension eased as the warm light dappled his skin where it pierced the overhead canopy.

He'd done his utmost to not bump into Theo all week. It hadn't been that hard to do. With Theo busy with *Miller,* he'd been leaving his house early and getting back later than usual and they hadn't seen each other outside their shops either.

Hunter frowned.

Not that I'm keeping track of his comings and goings.

He inhaled the cool smell of pine and aspen and forced himself to relax. He loved nothing more than being outdoors and was determined not to let the man who'd occupied his every waking thought for the past week ruin his day.

The base of the cliffs appeared between the trees. There were already people scaling the rock face. Hunter waved and responded to the greetings he received as he stepped out of the cover of the forest.

Most of the rock climbing folks in Twilight Falls were customers of *Go Thomson!*

Imogen stood talking to someone a short distance away. The man had a helmet on and his back to Hunter.

Hunter slowed as he got closer. He'd know those shoulders anywhere.

As if sensing his stare, Theo turned. His mouth curved in a smile that sent butterflies fluttering through Hunter's stomach. "Hey."

"Er, hi." Hunter did his best not to stare.

He was fast realizing that Theo looked good in pretty much anything he wore. His current outfit was a short-sleeved T-shirt that exposed his toned, athletic arms and hugged his broad chest and washboard abs, and climbing pants that showcased his long legs and muscular thighs.

As usual, the man seemed oblivious to the attention of the female climbers around him.

"So, you're the lead climber?" Theo asked as Imogen handed Hunter his helmet.

"Yeah." Hunter put his hat on and secured his chin strap. "Imogen is relatively new at this, so we usually partner up. What about you?"

"I normally free climb when I'm on my own," Theo said.

They finished gearing up and headed over to a free section of the cliff.

"After you," Theo murmured to Hunter.

Imogen grinned.

Hunter cut his eyes sharply to her.

He was aware of Theo's gaze as he found a handhold and started to ascend; for some reason, he couldn't help but shake the feeling that Theo was staring at his ass.

Hunter soon succumbed to the rhythm of the climb, his muscles warming as he scaled the bluff and placed nuts and cams along the route Imogen would follow, his attention fully on the task at hand. He paused some time later, fixed an auto-locking belay device and carabiner to an anchor point in the rock, and looked down.

Theo was already more than half way up along a parallel route on his left.

Hunter blinked as he observed his confident movements.

He's good.

"Hunter, am I okay to go?" Imogen shouted from below.

"Yeah, you can come up now."

Hunter fed the climbing rope slowly through the belay system while Imogen started to climb, steadily removing the slack so as to keep her ascent stable. She was fifty feet off the ground when an alarmed shout came from above them.

"Rock!"

Hunter's stomach clenched. He tightened his brake hand on the rope, braced himself, and glanced below him. Imogen kept her head down as she'd been taught to do, her knuckles white where she gripped the rock wall.

Dirt and pebbles rained down around Hunter as the unseen loose rocks fell past him. Something hit his helmet hard. He gritted his teeth and hung on.

The cry he'd hope not to hear came from below a second later.

"Falling!" Imogen yelled.

Hunter grunted and leaned back, taking her weight on the rope as the auto-locking device on the belay kicked in. He fed the slack when she swung back toward the cliff and lowered her to the ground as fast and as safely as he could.

An ominous sound reached his ears just as her feet touched the dirt.

Hunter looked up.

The anchor point was coming loose from the cliff. His stomach lurched when he sagged suddenly. One of the cams shifted in the crack where he'd wedged it.

Fear gripped Hunter. He crimped his fingers and

wedged his toes in some cracks a second before the anchor gave way.

"Hunter!" Imogen screamed from below.

Hunter swallowed as he hung on grimly to the cliff face, his heart thumping hard.

"It's okay!" he yelled. "I'm alright."

There was movement below and to his left. Hunter looked over. His eyes widened.

Theo was headed determinedly toward him. He stopped a foot away a moment later, his breaths coming slightly fast.

"I'm going to lower you down."

Hunter swallowed. "I've got another auto-lock in my pouch."

Theo reached across and carefully removed the device from Hunter's bag while Imogen rapidly set up a belay on his line from below. He put a second belay together, clipped Hunter's rope to his harness, and performed a safety check.

"Ready?"

Hunter nodded, his racing pulse slowing as he met Theo's calm gaze. He glanced at Imogen before looking up the cliff face. A couple of the climbers were coming down to help them. Though Hunter would have loved to give them time to reach her, he knew he needed to move.

"Theo?"

"Yeah?"

"I'll free climb as much as I can."

Theo's eyes softened. "I've got you."

Hunter took a shallow breath and started to descend, fully focused on the rock face and where to place his feet and hands. His arms and legs were aching by the time he neared the ground, having lost his grip and footing only twice.

Theo had caught him expertly both times.

A gasp came somewhere above Hunter, the sound reaching him on the wind. The rope in his harness suddenly grew slack. He looked up, horrified.

Theo had fallen some fifteen feet before managing to secure himself on the cliff.

Imogen grunted as she leaned back and absorbed Theo's weight. She cried out when her legs came off the ground.

Theo slammed into the cliff.

Hunted jumped the last ten feet. The shock of the landing jarred his knees. He rose, stumbled toward Imogen, and caught the brake rope just as it slid through her grip. His hands trembled as he rapidly swapped the belay to his own harness and took the slack of the rope.

"I'm lowering you!" he shouted to Theo.

It was only when Theo reached the ground safely that Hunter saw the bloodied scrapes on his right arm and the awkward way he was holding it.

CHAPTER 11

"I'M SORRY," IMOGEN MUMBLED.

Theo shrugged where he sat having his broken forearm put in a cast.

"It was no one's fault. I'm just glad neither of you got hurt."

They were in the ER of the local hospital. Remorse filled Hunter when he met Theo's gaze.

"Thank you," he said quietly. "For saving me."

Theo was about to reply when the doctor walked into the treatment room.

"I reckon you'll be out of that in about four weeks," she said briskly. "You are as fit as a horse and the X-ray shows it was a clean break. I'm giving you a prescription for pain meds."

Imogen chewed her lower lip anxiously. "Will there be any long term effects?"

The doctor shook her head as she scribbled on a prescription pad. "Nah. He should be able to resume all activities as normal once the cast is off." She paused and gave Imogen a shrewd look. "Although, I'd be careful about sex for a while."

Imogen's eyes rounded. She glanced from Hunter to Theo, her face reddening.

"I'm not with him."

The doctor stared. "Oh. I see." She smiled at Theo and narrowed her eyes slightly at Hunter. "You're gonna have to do it cowgirl style for a while."

Hunter blinked, shocked.

Imogen muffled a snort behind a hand. The ER nurse bit her lip as she finished applying the cast, her shoulders shaking.

"Why is everyone assuming I'd be the bottom?" Hunter muttered in an outraged voice.

Theo chuckled at his disgruntled expression.

THE SEATBELT TIGHTENED SLIGHTLY ACROSS THEO'S CHEST when the Jeep rolled to a stop. He opened his eyes and looked around groggily.

The sun was sinking behind the mountains that loomed above the forests encircling the estate where he and Hunter lived. Hunter had parked in his driveway and was looking at him anxiously from where he sat in the driver's seat.

"How are you feeling? I was worried when you fell asleep."

"I'm okay." Theo rubbed a hand down his face and willed away the drowsiness from the pain killers.

He hadn't wanted to take them but Hunter and

Imogen had insisted he did while they got his car back to his house.

"Why don't I make you dinner and get you settled in for the night?"

Theo masked his surprise at Hunter's proposal.

He knew Hunter was feeling guilty about what happened today but he'd spoken the truth when he'd told him and Imogen that it was nobody's fault.

"Sure."

Theo fished his house keys out of his trousers and gave them to Hunter. Hunter came round his side of the Jeep to make sure he got down okay and hovered close to him while they climbed the steps to his lodge and went through the front door.

Theo bit back a smile.

He's like a mother hen.

Hunter looked around curiously as Theo flicked on the light in the foyer.

"This place is nice."

"Yeah. It came fully furnished." Theo guided Hunter through the living room and dining room and into a large kitchen that overlooked a pleasantly landscaped yard backing onto thick woodland. "Bar my clothes and climbing gear, I only brought a couple of items from my home."

Hunter crossed the room and opened the refrigerator.

"You haven't got a lot in here," he muttered with a small frown.

Theo grimaced. "Sorry, I've been meaning to get groceries. Things have been rather hectic at the shop."

"I have a couple of steaks and salad at home," Hunter said tentatively. "Why don't I go get them?"

"That sounds great." Theo paused. "Could you, er, maybe help me out of my clothes first? I want to take a shower."

Hunter blinked at that.

Theo did his best to keep a straight face. He was more than capable of taking his clothes off. He just couldn't resist the opportunity to be in such close quarters with Hunter.

"Sure," Hunter mumbled, his tone reluctant.

Theo led the way up the stairs and into his bedroom. He switched the light on, stopped by the bed, and turned to face Hunter.

Hunter glanced at the bed and hesitated before coming closer. His breath washed across Theo's throat as he grabbed hold of the hem of Theo's T-shirt. Theo studied him surreptitiously while he carefully peeled the item off his body, making sure not to snag it on the cast.

His eyelashes are long. And he has freckles on his nose.

Hunter swallowed and stared at Theo's chest and six-pack. His gaze dropped apprehensively to Theo's pants.

Theo bit his lower lip hard.

Hunter caught the gesture and scowled. "You're really enjoying this, aren't you?"

"I can't deny that I am," Theo admitted in a strangled voice.

Hunter looked surprised by his confession. His expression grew resolute.

"Let's do this."

Theo was about to tell him it was only a pair of pants

when Hunter's fingers brushed against his lower abdomen. He sucked in air at the contact, startled by how good it felt.

Hunter snatched his hand away and looked up, alarmed. "Sorry! Did that hurt?"

"Hmm, no," Theo murmured.

Hunter flushed when he registered the swelling in Theo's groin.

There was no way Theo could mask his growing arousal.

Hunter clenched his jaw, unbuttoned Theo's pants, and slid the material down his legs. Theo suppressed a groan as Hunter's hands skimmed his hot skin, his touch featherlight. He stepped out of the trousers.

Hunter's gaze locked on Theo's now impressive erection where it dented his boxers.

"Can you manage those?" he said gruffly.

"I don't think I can," Theo lied.

A muscle danced in Hunter's cheek. He grabbed the waistband of Theo's underwear and carefully moved it down Theo's hips and thighs, his face scant inches from Theo's thick cock.

Desire stormed through Theo when he saw the bulge in Hunter's pants.

He's turned on too.

Hunter avoided looking at Theo's groin and stepped back.

"I'll go get those steaks," he mumbled before practically running out of the bedroom. The sound of the front door slamming shut came seconds later.

Theo sighed and glanced at his raging erection.

"Cold shower it is, then," he muttered.

By the time Hunter returned, Theo had finished in the bathroom. He debated calling downstairs to ask Hunter to help him get dressed but thought that would be pushing his luck too far.

HUNTER TENSED WHEN HE HEARD THEO'S FOOTSTEPS ON the stairs.

The fresh smell of Theo's body wash filled the room as he entered the kitchen.

Hunter clamped down on his libido and kept his head firmly stuck in the cabinet he was busy exploring. It was bad enough that he'd had to strip Theo naked and had those sinful images permanently imprinted on the back of his mind. Now the damn man was traipsing about emitting the most divine scent and it was turning all of Hunter's buttons on, whether he liked it or not.

"What are you looking for?" Theo asked lightly.

And then, there's that voice. Why the hell does he always sound like he'd just had sex?!

"A skillet," Hunter replied stiffly.

There was movement behind him. Hunter straightened, startled.

Theo opened the cabinet next to him and removed a frying pan.

Hunter turned. "Thanks."

"You're welcome."

Hunter gazed at Theo's gray sweatpants and black T-shirt and tried not to think of the hard angles and sculptured muscles beneath them. He narrowed his eyes.

"I see you had no difficulty getting yourself dressed."

Theo smiled. "I broke my left arm once when I was a teenager, so I know all the tricks."

Hunter gave him an incensed look. "So you all out lied to me?!"

"I didn't exactly lie. And, let's face it." Theo stepped closer. "I'd be a fool not to try and take advantage of this situation a little bit."

Hunter froze when he found himself trapped between the cabinet and Theo.

Theo's eyes grew hooded. He lowered his gaze to Hunter's mouth.

"Theo?" Hunter mumbled.

"Yeah?" Theo leaned in slightly, his lips stopping scant inches from Hunter's.

"The skillet," Hunter said hoarsely.

He snatched the frying pan from Theo's grasp and slipped away.

"Chicken," Theo chuckled in his wake.

CHAPTER 12

He's going to make me lose my mind.

Hunter climbed the porch to Theo's front door, knocked, and waited nervously.

Dinner last night had been more enjoyable than he'd thought it would be. Once Theo backed off and stopped trying to make a move on him, they'd spent a couple of surprisingly pleasant hours talking about life, their jobs, and their friends. It turned out Theo wasn't only a close friend of the owner of the gay club where they'd met in L.A., but was also the guy's rock climbing buddy. And Hunter discovered that Theo was not just good looking, but was witty, charming, and intelligent to boot.

He grimaced.

So, basically, all the things I like in a guy.

Hunter pursed his lips, jammed his hands in the pockets of his jeans, and rocked back on his heels. He was going to have to be extra careful around Theo from now, or else he'd succumb to the man's charms.

He feared he would lose more than just his role as a top if that were to happen.

The door opened. Theo appeared, smelling as heavenly as always. He was wearing a white shirt, navy pants, and a light blue blazer thrown on his oh-so-broad shoulders and over his sling and cast.

Hunter bit back a sigh.

Yup, I'm definitely in trouble.

"Thanks for giving me a lift to work," Theo said as they headed for the Jeep, oblivious to the dangerous direction Hunter's thoughts had just taken.

"It's the least I can do," Hunter murmured.

He'd told Theo he would chauffeur him to his shop and around town while he couldn't drive, with Imogen acting as their backup. He started the engine and drove out of the estate, acutely conscious of Theo's presence beside him.

Here's hoping I survive the next few weeks.

THEO FROWNED AS HE APPROACHED *MILLER*. THE FRONT windows of the store looked strangely bare. He quickened his steps, Hunter trailing in his wake. They entered the shop and found a distressed Codie standing in the middle of the floor, next to a rack of clothes and a pile of boxes.

As the manager, Codie kept the same working hours as Theo, often arriving before he did and leaving well after the other staff had gone home. Theo had suspected he'd be the first in this morning too, considering only a week had passed since the store's grand opening.

"What's going on?" Hunter said curiously behind him.

"I don't know," Theo murmured.

Codie's face cleared when he saw Theo. "Thank God you're here! We have an emergency!" His gaze dropped to Theo's cast. Horror filled his face. "What happened?" He rushed over. "Are you okay?!"

"I'm fine." Theo waved his good hand dismissively. "What's wrong?"

"So, I took down the stock we used for our opening week and sent it back to L.A. on Saturday night, like we'd planned. But the shipment we were waiting for to finish dressing the windows with our late summer-early autumn stock hasn't arrived," Codie explained anxiously. "Kate ordered it weeks ago, but I just got a phone call from the delivery company and they said it won't be here until the afternoon. Kate said she'd come over as soon as she can with some spare inventory from the L.A. store, but I'm not sure she'll make it in time."

Theo frowned. This was definitely not the kind of news he wanted to hear when they were only in the second week of their launch.

"We have plenty of merchandise out back, so we'll have to do with those. It's not ideal, but it's the best we can do under the circumstances."

Codie nodded. "That's what I thought too. Can you help me choose what we should put out front?" He indicated the clothes and the boxes behind him. "Kate gave me a plan for how she wanted things laid out for the original shipment."

"Sure." Theo gave him a reassuring smile. "I've learned a thing or two from Kate over the years."

"Do you guys need a hand?" Hunter said.

Theo and Codie exchanged a surprised glance.

"Are you sure?" Theo asked. "You've got your own place to manage."

Codie hesitated. "And you'd be helping the, er, enemy."

Hunter rolled his eyes. "Imogen can manage the shop. And if you guys think you'll be able to put me out of business just like that, you've got another thing coming. Besides, I do the window dressing for *Go Thomson!*"

Theo and Codie stared.

Hunter arched an eyebrow. "Why are you guys looking at me like that?"

"Well—" Theo started.

"Your outfit is kinda, hmm—" Codie mumbled.

Hunter looked down at his sneakers, jeans, and T-shirt.

"What's wrong with my outfit?" he said defensively.

"It's…casual," Theo said in a diplomatic voice. "To be frank, I assumed Imogen was your display designer when I saw you two in the window a couple of weeks ago."

Hunter narrowed his eyes. "Look, do you want a hand or not?"

The corner of Theo's mouth quirked up in amusement at Hunter's irate expression. Hunter all riled up was sexy as hell too.

"We would love your help."

Hunter called Imogen to tell her he'd be late coming over and opened up the boxes Codie had brought from out back. He examined the array of clothes and accessories on hand before gazing pensively around the shop.

"Have you got pictures of your other stores?" he asked Theo.

"Sure."

Theo pulled his cell phone out and brought up photos of the other *Miller* branches. Hunter came closer and peered at the screen. The minty scent of his shampoo wafted tantalizing across Theo's nose.

I wonder if his skin smells like that too.

Theo ignored the stirring in his groin and did his best to focus on the problem at hand. They had an hour left until *Miller* opened for its second week of business.

Hunter and Codie got to work, Theo helping as much as he could with his broken arm.

They stood on the curb some forty minutes later and examined their handiwork.

"What do you think?" Hunter said critically.

"It looks great," Theo said, surprised.

Hunter had arranged the windows to match the style of the other *Miller* stores. He'd also added his own personal twist to showcase some of the sports apparel Theo and Kate had recently added to their inventory.

"You sound shocked," Hunter said in a dry voice.

Theo grinned. "I kinda am. You're really good at this."

Hunter's ears reddened at the compliment.

Codie glanced curiously between the two of them.

A blue Porsche raced up the road and pulled in sharply a few cars ahead of where they stood. Kate stepped out, looking harassed and breathless. She removed several clothes bags from the trunk and headed over briskly toward the store.

"Hey! I'm here!" She blew a stray lock of blonde hair

from her flushed face. "How did you guys manage to dress the windows? They look fantastic." She stopped when she saw Hunter. Astonishment flared on her face. "Er, isn't that—"

"Hunter, this is Kate Vincent, my business partner," Theo interrupted smoothly while Codie went to help her. "Kate, this is Hunter Thomson, the owner of *Go Thomson!* He helped me and Codie out."

"Hi," Hunter said with a dip of his chin.

Kate was speechless for a moment, a feat Theo knew was rare. The look she gave him indicated there would be questions later. She gave the clothes bags to Codie and came over to shake Hunter's hand.

"Thank you. We really appreciate that."

"No problem," Hunter murmured.

Kate frowned at Theo's cast. "What happened to your arm?"

"It's a long story."

CHAPTER 13

HUNTER WAS CONSCIOUS OF IMOGEN'S CURIOUS STARE when he entered their office just after opening time.

"How's Theo?" she asked.

"He's good." Hunter plopped down on his chair and put his feet up on the desk.

Imogen raised an eyebrow. "I saw you helping them with their window display."

"They had an emergency," Hunter said guiltily. "Besides, we owe him."

"I know. And I didn't mean it that way." Imogen sighed. "I'm popping out to get breakfast pastries from Elijah's place. Wanna a coffee?"

"Sure."

Hunter's cell buzzed a moment later. It was Theo.

Theo: How about I treat you to dinner tonight as a thank you for this morning?

Hunter hesitated before tapping out a reply.

Hunter: You don't have to.

His phone vibrated in his hand.

Theo: I insist. You're a lifesaver. I'll let you pick the place.

Hunter's lips tilted in a faint smile.

This guy really doesn't know the meaning of the word "No".

He messaged Theo back.

Hunter: Okay.

The day went faster than Hunter thought it would. Despite *Miller* opening opposite, *Go Thomson!* remained as busy as always. He kept a discreet eye on the store across the road when he relieved Imogen behind the counter and was glad to see it was still full of people.

He had no doubt Theo's place would be a hit with the folks of Twilight Falls, especially after having handled their stock that morning. He could tell how much thought Theo and Kate had put into the materials they'd sourced and the designers they'd used to represent their brand.

"That's the fifth time you've looked at your watch in as many minutes."

Hunter startled and looked over his shoulder.

Imogen was leaning in the doorway of their office and watching him with a shrewd expression. "If I didn't know any better, I'd say you have a date."

Hunter felt his cheeks grow warm.

Imogen stared. "Wait. You have a date?!"

"Who's got a date?" Benji chirped from the shop floor.

To Hunter's relief, their store was empty. There was only half an hour left till closing time.

"It's not a date," he muttered. "Theo's just taking me out for dinner to thank me for helping him out."

Imogen sucked in air. Benji gaped.

"Whoa," Chloe murmured, her eyes round.

Hunter frowned at their expressions. "Like I said, it's not a date."

"Sure," Imogen said in an indulgent voice.

Benji smirked. "Whatever you say, boss."

"Right," Chloe added, clearly unconvinced.

Despite his best efforts, Hunter found himself counting down the time until they closed up. Benji and Chloe left first and he saw off Imogen a short while after. He was tidying up behind the counter when the front door of *Go Thomson!* opened.

Hunter's pulse accelerated when Theo walked in.

"How was your day?" he blurted out to hide his nervousness.

Theo blinked and slowed at the abrupt question. Hunter silently cursed himself.

Dammit. Why am I so jumpy?!

A dazzling smile curved Theo's mouth. Hunter's stomach flip-flopped.

Ah, shit.

"It was great," Theo said, unaware of the longing storming over Hunter. "Thanks again for everything. Kate was really impressed by your design style."

"It was nothing," Hunter protested weakly.

Theo cocked his head, his expression puzzled. He'd obviously picked up on Hunter's odd mood. "Are you ready?"

Hunter nodded jerkily. "Yeah. Just give me a minute. I'll grab my jacket."

He turned and headed into his office, his legs suddenly weak. He stopped by his desk and pressed a hand to his chest.

His heart was thumping hard against his ribs.

"Jesus, calm down," Hunter muttered to himself. "You're just having dinner with the guy."

"Hunter?"

Hunter whipped round.

Theo had followed him into the office.

"What—what are you doing here?" Hunter stammered, flustered.

"I was worried about you." Theo came closer. "You're acting kinda strange. Are you okay?"

No, I'm not. You're driving me crazy.

Theo's eyes flared with awareness. "I am?"

Hunter groaned when he realized he'd said the words out loud. He rubbed a hand down his face.

"I want to crawl into a hole in the ground so badly right now."

Amusement lit Theo's gaze. His expression turned serious once more.

He stepped toward Hunter.

Hunter backed away. His butt hit the edge of his desk a heartbeat later.

"Uh-oh." Theo stopped in front of Hunter. "Looks like you've run out of places to hide, Kitty Kat."

Blood pounded rapidly in Hunter's veins. He could feel his earlobes pulsing with the fast beat. Theo's intoxicating scent had wrapped around him and was threatening to drown his senses.

"Kitty Kat?" Hunter breathed.

"Yup." Theo dipped his chin. "You remind me of a cat. All aloof and defensive."

Hunter tried to maintain a hold on his rapidly fading sanity.

"I'm not sure I appreciate that comparison. It makes me sound tame."

Theo leaned in. "And you're not? Tame?"

Hunter hesitated before shaking his head, his gaze dropping briefly to Theo's mouth.

Theo's eyes darkened. "So, I drive you crazy, huh?"

Hunter licked his lips and swallowed nervously. "Yeah."

Theo's pupils dilated. "Good. 'Cause you drive me crazy too," he confessed huskily, his eyes on Hunter's mouth. "So much so all I can think about these days is you."

Oh God.

CHAPTER 14

THEO KNEW THE SECOND HUNTER SURRENDERED TO THE attraction sizzling between them. A hungry sound left Hunter as he closed the scant distance separating their bodies. His lips clashed with Theo's at the same time he clasped Theo's head and sank his fingers demandingly in Theo's hair.

Theo groaned at Hunter's kiss.

He could feel Hunter's desire in the way he was moulding his mouth and body to Theo's, and his racing heartbeat where it thundered wildly against Theo's chest.

Hunter wanted him. Badly.

Theo maneuvered Hunter until he was sitting on the edge of his desk, moved into the cradle of Hunter's thighs, and looped his good arm around Hunter's back.

Hunter seemed oblivious to it all, his attention focused on where he was boldly invading Theo's mouth. He wrapped his tongue around Theo's own hot flesh.

Theo pressed their bodies close, his cock throbbing as

his passion for the man in his arms escalated rapidly. He took over the kiss.

Hunter gasped when Theo masterfully frenched him, sucking and nibbling and lashing at his tongue, the wet sounds of their mating flesh echoing around the room and arousing both of them.

Theo dropped his good hand to Hunter's belt and quickly undid the buckle.

The needy sound Hunter made and the way he gripped Theo's hips with his thighs told him he thoroughly approved of the action. He lowered his own hands to Theo's pants and did the same, his neck arching as he pressed his greedy mouth up to Theo's.

Theo freed Hunter's erection and groaned when Hunter's hand closed on his own straining shaft. They started stroking one another, their movements jerky and fast.

"Oh God," Hunter moaned. "That feels fucking good!"

Theo gazed hotly into Hunter's passion-glazed eyes and circled his thumb teasingly across the sensitive head of Hunter's cock, spreading the hot precum oozing from his shivering shaft. Hunter gasped and twitched, one hand rising to grasp Theo's shoulder in a punishing grip.

"Jesus!"

Hunter panted against Theo's lips and accelerated the motion of his own hand on Theo's rock hard erection as Theo pleasured him.

Theo reluctantly wrenched his mouth from Hunter's and looked down to where they were rubbing each other's dicks. He cursed at the bewitching sight of his hand on

Hunter's flushed cock, dropped down on his knees, and took Hunter in his mouth.

~

"*OH!*"

Hunter sucked in air, shocked by Theo's unexpected move.

He lowered his gaze dazedly and groaned at the sinful sight of Theo going down on him. Theo met his hot stare, his hazel eyes green with passion as he sucked and licked Hunter's cock, his good hand locked on Hunter's right thigh to keep him in place.

Hunter shivered and bit his lower lip hard when the first wave of his orgasm swirled deliciously through his belly and thighs. His head fell back and he started punching his hips, unable to stop his body's natural urge to fuck the mouth pleasuring him. He pressed one hand on the desk behind him and weaved the fingers of the other in Theo's thick hair.

Theo grunted and bobbed his head in tandem with Hunter's thrusts, taking him deeper and deeper into the scorching depths of his throat.

Hunter stiffened a moment later, eyes closing and mouth opening on a harsh cry as he crested the heady rise of his climax. The most intense pleasure exploded inside him. He convulsed violently, his heels digging in Theo's back at the same time he lifted his butt off the desk and shoved his pulsing cock repeatedly inside Theo's ravenous mouth. Low keens and moans reached him dully through the blood pounding in his skull. It took a moment to realize he was the one making those noises.

Hunter panted and went limp as he navigated the warm, blissful shores of his afterglow, his ass and balls twitching with the fading pulses of his orgasm.

An animal sound made him blink his eyes open.

Hunter looked down and stilled when he saw Theo's face.

Theo slowly let go of Hunter's achingly spent cock and kept his eyes on him as he jerked his own hips, his good hand working his dick toward his own climax, his expression feverish.

Heat flooded Hunter as he watched the erotic display. He couldn't have looked away from the man pleasuring himself so wantonly before him even if he'd wanted to.

Theo's mouth parted on a hard groan when he came, his cum splashing onto his hand and the floor.

"Hunter!" he gasped.

The sound of his name on Theo's lips while he shuddered and shook in the throes of his potent orgasm was Hunter's final undoing. He surrendered to temptation, cradled Theo's face in his hands, and leaned down to take Theo's mouth in a sultry kiss. Theo responded hungrily.

Hunter moaned when he tasted himself on Theo's lips and tongue. He pressed his forehead against Theo's sweat-slicked brow as Theo finally relaxed down onto the floor.

Shivers shook Theo, the aftershocks of his climax still coursing through him.

Their heated pants filled the room as they stared at one another.

"Wow," Theo whispered.

"Like I said," Hunter murmured. "You drive me crazy."

Theo nibbled on Hunter's lower lip and nuzzled their noses together. "It makes me happy to hear you say that." A sexy smile split his mouth. "How about we have dinner and do this again?"

Hunter narrowed his eyes. "Not happening." He straightened. "I said you drive me crazy. I didn't say I intended to do something about it." He tucked his dick back inside his jeans and zipped himself up.

Theo stared. "Sure." He climbed to his feet and cleaned his hand with a tissue.

Hunter scowled. "You don't sound convinced."

Theo pursed his lips.

"Are you laughing at me?" Hunter growled.

"I'm not," Theo protested in a strangled voice.

"I can and I *will* resist whatever this—this thing is between us!" Hunter stated mutinously. He stabbed a finger in Theo's chest. "I'm not falling for your charms again!"

"Whatever you say, Kitty Kat," Theo drawled, clearly amused.

"And stop calling me that!"

Theo grinned at Hunter's scowl. "So, where are we going for dinner?"

CHAPTER 15

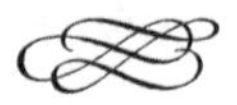

"THANK GOD IT'S NEARLY SUNDAY," HUNTER GROANED.

Imogen looked at him curiously. "What's up?"

"Nothing," Hunter said where he sat balancing the accounts for the week. "Just looking forward to some R&R."

He could hardly admit to Imogen that he'd spent most of the week in a state of near permanent arousal. Though Theo hadn't made any further advances toward him since the day they'd given each other hand jobs and Theo had blown him to a spectacular orgasm in this very office, Hunter couldn't help but feel that Theo was biding his time and slowly chipping away at his defenses with a charm offensive.

And Hunter found himself not minding it all that terribly.

Christ, it's almost as if I want *him to make a move on me.*

Driving Theo to and from work and into town on the odd occasion he'd needed to get something had become both the highlight and the bane of Hunter's day. It was hard to maintain his distance from the man when they were at such close quarters. And, however much he wanted to dismiss the magnetic pull between them, there was no denying that he was very much attracted to Theo.

Theo had kept their conversations light and friendly this past week, to the point Hunter wondered if he'd actually forgotten about what had transpired between them a few evenings ago. Something twisted in Hunter's chest at that thought.

Though he had yet to give Theo a clear answer about his own feelings, Hunter didn't want Theo to give up on them just yet. He was busy digesting that sobering thought when the entrance door jangled in the distance.

"I thought you put the 'Closed' sign up," Imogen said.

"I did. It might be Theo coming over early."

Hunter ignored his skittering pulse and headed out of the office. A strange mixture of disappointment and relief swept over him when he saw the trio on the other side of the counter. He stopped and frowned.

"I thought poker night was canceled."

"It is," Tristan said. "I was heading home when I bumped into these two." He cocked a thumb at Wyatt and his younger sister, Izzy Batista.

Izzy smiled. "Wyatt and I were planning to catch dinner before heading home. Four sounded merrier than three, so we thought we'd come get you."

"I'm afraid I can't," Hunter said. "I have an errand to run."

He was hardly going to admit to them that his errand

was over six foot two, with piercing hazel eyes and a killer face and body.

Izzy's face fell. "You do?"

Guilt flashed through Hunter.

Izzy looked past him. "Oh. Hi, Imogen."

Imogen came up behind Hunter.

"Hey, Izzy. What are you guys doing here?"

"We were picking up Hunter for dinner. Wanna come? He says he needs to run an errand."

"He does?" Imogen raised an eyebrow at Hunter. "I thought you were giving Theo a lift home?"

Tristan stiffened.

"Who's Theo?" Izzy said.

Wyatt shook his head and made a frantic mouth-zipping motion behind his sister.

Hunter scowled. He didn't have to be told to keep Theo's identity a secret from Izzy. Wyatt's kid sister had been the scourge of the Terrible Seven's lives ever since she joined them in junior high. She was nosy, butted into their affairs on a regular basis, and generally thought she knew what was best for all of them.

Irritatingly enough, she was right most of the time.

The shop door jangled open again. Theo strolled in, looking gorgeous in charcoal slacks, a white shirt, and a forest green blazer that matched his eyes and his dress shoes.

Hunter swallowed a groan. *Great.*

Imogen's face brightened. "Hey, Theo."

Tristan frowned at Theo.

Hunter bit back a sigh. He could tell his best friend had just gone into protective mode.

Theo greeted Imogen with a nod before glancing apologetically between Hunter and the trio gathered before the counter.

"Sorry, I thought you'd closed."

"It's okay," Hunter said. "These are some friends of mine. And they were just leaving." He gave Tristan, Wyatt, and Izzy a pointed stare.

Tristan ignored him and continued glowering at Theo.

Theo gave the mechanic a puzzled look.

"Why so cold?" Izzy asked Hunter curiously.

Imogen pursed her lips and looked surreptitiously from Hunter to Theo.

A sharp light dawned in Izzy's eyes when she caught Imogen's glance.

Hunter almost swore when she turned to Theo and flashed a bright smile at him.

"Hi, I'm Izzy. This is my brother, Wyatt. And this is Tristan, Hunter's best friend."

Theo shook her hand, slightly bemused. "Theo Miller."

"Oh!" Izzy exclaimed. "As in the guy who owns the new store?"

"The very one." Theo studied Tristan's stormy expression and offered him a hand. "Nice to meet you."

Tristan hesitated before shaking it gruffly.

Theo chuckled when Tristan released his hand. "Whoa. That's a strong grip." He exchanged handshakes with an apologetic looking Wyatt, the amused light dancing in his eyes indicating he knew full well Tristan had just tried to intimidate him with brute strength.

Hunter gave Tristan a *I-can't-believe-you-just-did-that* glare.

Tristan didn't look in the least bit abashed by his bullish behavior.

Izzy cocked her head at Theo's cast and sling with a sympathetic grimace. "I take it the reason Hunter is driving you home is because of your broken arm?"

"Yes," Theo replied in a light tone. "I moved in opposite Hunter a few weeks ago, so it's pretty easy for him to give me a lift to and from work."

"You're renting the place opposite Hunter?" Tristan grumbled.

Theo eyed Tristan steadily. "I am."

"It's because of us that Theo broke his arm," Imogen explained guiltily.

Izzy stared. "Now, that sounds like the kind of story that should be told over food and drinks." She hooked an arm through the crook of Theo's left elbow. "How about you join us for dinner?"

"Theo needs to go home," Hunter stated mutinously.

"Yeah, I don't think this is a great idea," Tristan fairly growled.

Izzy narrowed her eyes at Tristan. "Down, Cujo." She looked from Hunter to Theo and back. "It's clear there's something going on between you guys. Mama wants deets." She started dragging Theo toward the exit.

The first sign of unease appeared on Theo's face. He glanced at Hunter. "Er, Hunter?"

"I'm so sorry, man," Wyatt muttered to Theo.

Imogen patted Hunter lightly on the back as Izzy tugged a reluctant Theo along, Tristan and Wyatt following slowly in their wake. "Good luck. I'd loved to come and save your ass, but I promised Deacon we'd go for a drink tonight. I hope the Batista Inquisition doesn't kill you."

"Thanks," Hunter muttered.

CHAPTER 16

"WHOA! SO, YOU GUYS SHACKED UP IN L.A. OVER A MONTH ago?" Izzy blinked in amazement. "And you saved Hunter's life last weekend?!"

Heads turned across the busy restaurant.

"Will you keep your voice down?" Hunter hissed at Izzy, his ears reddening under the battery of avid stares they were attracting.

Theo swallowed a strangled chuckle behind his good hand. Wyatt sighed.

Tristan scowled at Hunter. "How come you didn't tell me about the accident?"

"'Cause I've been busy," Hunter snapped. He turned to Izzy. "And we didn't shack up. It was a one-time thing and it's not happening again!"

Theo arched an eyebrow. "Really?"

He kept his expression neutral, not sure whether it was disappointment or irritation he was feeling at Hunter's stubborn words.

Hunter gave him a defiant look. "Yeah. The *incident*

from Monday doesn't count."

The way Hunter looked away at the last second told Theo this was a boldfaced lie.

"Oooh, now that sounds juicy," Izzy murmured.

Wyatt hushed her.

Theo took a leisurely sip of his wine and met Hunter's eyes steadily. "You're forgetting our kiss the week I turned up in Twilight Falls. And the one we shared at the bar."

A muscle danced in Hunter's cheek.

Theo masked a smile behind his glass.

My cat is cute when he's angry. He's also far too obstinate for his own good.

"Monday's incident was fun," Theo continued in a low drawl, deliberately dropping his voice an octave. "Really fun. In fact, I can't remember the last time I…enjoyed myself so much. Except for that time in L.A., of course."

Hunter's pupils flared at his husky tone. He frowned in the next instant.

Theo bit back a laugh. He could tell Hunter wasn't immune to his voice and was currently reliving the insanely hot minutes they'd spent pleasuring each other in his office. He was also willing to bet a lot of money that Hunter was aroused right now.

A crunch distracted him.

Izzy had grabbed a carrot stick from Wyatt's plate and was munching on it, her fascinated stare swinging between Theo and Hunter.

"Holy shit," she mumbled. "There's enough sexual chemistry between you two to put my hair on end. Please, carry on."

Hunter groaned and dropped his head in his hands.

"Please do something about your sister," he begged Wyatt.

"I'm afraid that ship sailed twenty-eight years ago," Wyatt muttered.

Theo grinned. Izzy's words should have vexed him. After all, what was happening between him and Hunter only concerned the two of them. Except Hunter's circle of friends seemed pretty determined to have a say in his love life. And it was evident from their dynamics that they were highly protective of one another.

Theo could tell Izzy wasn't being nosy for the sake of it, but because she genuinely cared for Hunter and wanted him to be safe and happy. He found himself very much enjoying the company of Hunter's friends. He even liked the grouchy Tristan, who hadn't stopped glaring at him once since they left Hunter's store.

It was clear to Theo that Tristan would happily put his life on the line for Hunter. And, despite having only just met the man, Theo was pretty confident it wasn't because Tristan had any kind of romantic interest in Hunter.

If anything, Tristan was acting like Hunter's big brother.

Theo decided honesty was going to be the best policy when it came to dealing to Hunter's friends. And with Hunter himself.

"You're right," Theo admitted. "I can't deny that I like Hunter. A lot."

Hunter flushed where he sat opposite him.

"Yowza." Izzy snatched another carrot stick from under her brother's nose and waved it at Theo. "So, it's pretty serious, huh?"

Theo locked eyes with Hunter.

"I would like it to be," he said quietly. "I've made it clear to Hunter how I feel about him."

Izzy sucked in air.

Wyatt paused, his fork halfway to his mouth. Tristan's hand froze on his glass.

Hunter's heart pounded in his chest at Theo's heartfelt expression. He could tell Theo was being deadly serious, just as he had been that night at *The Watering Hole* and the time he'd come to his place. He opened his mouth.

"I—"

Hunter faltered and stopped.

An awkward silence fell across their table. Hunter dug his nails into his palms and silently cursed himself.

He felt like an absolute cad.

"It's okay," Theo added. "I'm not expecting you to give me an answer right now."

How he made it through the rest of dinner, Hunter didn't know. Izzy, Wyatt, and Theo kept the conversation going while Hunter brooded over Theo's confession. Tristan gradually thawed and finally joined in near the end.

They parted ways outside the restaurant, Tristan's anxious gaze following Hunter and Theo as they headed back to where Hunter had parked his Jeep.

Hunter and Theo climbed inside the vehicle in silence.

"Want the radio on?" Hunter asked stiffly as he secured his seat belt.

"Sure," Theo replied quietly.

Hunter reached over to the dashboard and pressed a button. Low rock music echoed from the speakers.

Lines wrinkled Theo's brow as he struggled with his seat belt clip.

"Here, let me help," Hunter murmured.

Theo stilled as Hunter leaned over and slid a hand over his fingers before fastening his belt. "Thanks." His breath washed across the side of Hunter's face.

Hunter swallowed hard and moved back, his pulse hammering away. "No problem."

Theo's skin was hot enough to scald his fingertips.

Hunter pulled away from the curb.

They were almost at the estate when Theo spoke.

"I'm sorry."

Hunter glanced at him, surprised. "For what?"

"For putting you on the spot like that, especially in front of your friends."

Hunter's knuckles whitened on the steering wheel.

"I was serious," Theo continued. "About what I said."

Hunter was intensely aware of Theo where he sat next to him. Though he'd told himself he was still upset at Theo because the man had used his friend to boost his business, deep down inside, he knew this wasn't the truth. Hunter was conscious his frustration was founded in the complex feelings he was harboring for the man beside him. Feelings he wasn't ready to face yet.

He pulled into his driveway, turned the engine off, and frowned into the night.

Theo undid his seatbelt. "That's a mighty big scowl."

Hunter took a shuddering breath before twisting in his seat and staring at Theo.

"I'm angry. With myself. With you." He fisted his hands. "And I don't know why."

Theo went deathly still. "You don't know why?" he repeated after a taut silence. "Then maybe I should show you."

Theo closed the gap separating them, hooked his good hand around Hunter's nape, and pulled him in for a blistering kiss.

Hunter gasped and shivered. Desire slammed into him, so strong and heavy he felt like he'd gone under a wave. He raised trembling hands and buried them in Theo's hair, clinging on for dear life.

Theo murmured in approval and probed Hunter's lips with his hungry tongue.

Though Hunter could sense his smoldering impatience, Theo's touch was gentle where he cradled Hunter's neck. Hunter let out a breathy sigh and opened his mouth. A moan left him when Theo swooped inside.

They kissed for what felt like a lifetime, their breaths loud and fast in the enclosed space, the wet sounds of their mating flesh so arousing Hunter's cock twitched and hardened.

Theo finally wrenched his mouth from Hunter's and pressed their foreheads together. "You want me," he growled. "Just as badly as I want you. That's why you're so frustrated." He pulled back and took Hunter's chin in his warm fingers. "You know what I want to do right now?"

Hunter swallowed, his pulse hammering in his veins.

He could hazard a guess from the wild look on Theo's face.

"I want to touch you all over." Theo's hazel eyes were dark with passion as he gazed fiercely at Hunter. "I want to strip you bare and kiss you from your head to your toes. I want to blow your cock. I want to make you scream in pleasure. And I really, *really* want to have sex with you."

Hunter's breath froze in his throat. Theo's brazen confession had his heart thundering violently in his chest. No one had ever admitted their feelings for him the way Theo had just done. No one had ever bared their soul and their desires so openly to him before. And no one had ever made him feel as torn as Theo was making him feel right now.

"Let me make something clear." Theo pulled back and lowered his hand to his thigh.

Hunter's stomach twisted. He missed Theo's touch already.

"This is more than lust." Theo stared at Hunter hotly. "I don't just want your body, Hunter. I want your heart too." He opened the passenger door and stepped out into the night.

Hunter stared after him, his mind wracked with confusion and his soul in turmoil.

CHAPTER 17

Sleep over tonight.

Theo hesitated as he stared at the message he'd just typed out on his cell phone.

It had been two days since he and Hunter had kissed in his Jeep and he'd confessed his feelings to Hunter. Though Hunter had acted as if nothing had happened between them when he'd picked him up the next morning, Theo had detected the trace of reservation deep in his gray eyes and knew he was still thinking about what Theo had said to him.

Winning Hunter over was proving to be the biggest challenge of Theo's life. He suspected the reward, if he were to be successful, would be the sweetest victory he'd ever tasted.

Theo took a deep breath and pressed the send button.

He waited breathlessly for Hunter's reply. A minute passed, then two.

His cell buzzed with an incoming call. Theo's heart lurched.

It was Hunter.

Theo's fingers trembled as he answered.

"That's a bad idea," Hunter stated without preamble. "Like, super bad."

Theo couldn't stop the smile that split his mouth. He could imagine Hunter gnawing on his lip and frowning at the other end of the line. He decided to go in with all guns blazing.

"I like you, Hunter. I like you a lot. I know you have your own reservations about what's happening between us, but I've never felt this way about anyone before and I don't want to walk away from this."

Hunter inhaled sharply.

"I—I just can't!" he stammered after a short silence.

Theo frowned. "Because we're both tops?"

"Yes," Hunter admitted breathily.

Theo fell silent.

"Do you want to top me?" he finally said. "Because I don't mind if you—"

"No!" Hunter blurted out.

Theo blinked, surprised.

It seemed Hunter was similarly surprised by his outburst from his shocked pause.

"We don't have to have penetrative sex," Theo said. "There are a lot of gay couples who don't and still have a perfectly satisfactory relationship."

"I wouldn't be happy with that," Hunter mumbled. "And neither would you."

Theo leaned back in his chair. "Can I ask you a favor?"

Hunter swallowed audibly. "What is it?"

"Will you sleep over tonight?"

Hunter didn't reply.

"I just want to sleep next to you," Theo said. "I promise, I won't push you to do anything you don't want to do."

HUNTER USED THE SPARE KEY THEO HAD GIVEN HIM AFTER the accident and let himself inside Theo's house.

He paused inside the shadowy foyer, his heart thumping in his chest.

I can't believe I'm doing this.

The sound of the shower reached him as he started down the hall and neared the stairs. An image of a nude Theo under a spray of hot water flashed before his eyes.

Hunter's cock stirred. He groaned.

Down, boy.

Hunter waited until his burgeoning erection had abated before climbing the steps to Theo's bedroom.

Theo walked out of the en suite bathroom just as Hunter entered the room. He paused, one hand on the towel he was using to briskly dry his hair. A beguiling smile lit his face as he raked Hunter's T-shirt and checkered pajama bottoms with his gaze.

"I like your PJs."

"Thanks," Hunter muttered.

He was struggling to think straight and it had everything to do with the wickedly alluring man staring at him. Bar the dark sweatpants riding low on his hips, Theo was naked. And his heady scent was literally filling the bedroom.

Hunter fisted his hands.

He felt scared and breathless all of a sudden, as if he were standing on the edge of a precipice, about to fall.

He just wants to sleep next to me. We're not going to have sex.

Hunter's libido laughed at that.

"Want me to dry your hair?" he blurted.

Theo's eyes widened.

Hunter cursed internally.

Why the hell did I just say that?

"Er, sure," Theo murmured.

He disposed of the towel, removed a hair dryer from a drawer, and sat down on the Chesterfield chair by the window.

Hunter took the appliance from Theo and plugged it in a nearby outlet. Theo leaned his elbows on his knees and bowed his head. Hunter stepped in front to him and turned on the hairdryer.

Two minutes in and Hunter decided he had made a terrible mistake.

Theo's hair was as soft as silk. Not just that, but the smell of his shampoo and body wash were so intoxicating and the occasional hum of appreciation he uttered as Hunter caressed his scalp so electrifying Hunter's toes were literally curling in pleasure.

"There, all done," Hunter mumbled a short time later.

Theo blinked and looked at him dazedly as he stepped away.

"Thanks," he said huskily. "That was nice."

Theo's raspy voice made every nerve ending on Hunter's body tingle. He swallowed, unplugged the hair dryer, and put it on top of the dresser.

"Which side do you like to sleep on?"

Hunter whipped around.

Theo was standing to the left of the bed and holding up the edge of the comforter.

"I don't mind," Hunter murmured.

"Okay. Can you hit the main light?"

"Sure."

Hunter forced his racing pulse to slow down as he switched off the overhead light and crossed the dimly-lit bedroom. He climbed under the comforter, turned his back to Theo, and closed his eyes.

"Goodnight."

The mattress dipped slightly. Something warm and heavy sneaked around Hunter's waist. He stiffened.

"What are you doing?"

"There's not much point sleeping together if I can't touch you," Theo replied, tightening his arm around Hunter.

Hunter shivered as Theo's hot breath washed across his nape and ruffled his hair.

"That's cheating," he mumbled.

A low chuckle came behind him. "Goodnight, Hunter."

Hunter frowned.

Yeah, right. Like I'm going to be able to sleep now.

THEO SLOWLY BLINKED HIS EYES OPEN. PALE LIGHT PIERCED a narrow gap in the curtains and illuminated the bedroom with a faint glow. He could tell from the angle of the sun that it was still early. He started to stretch and stilled when something heavy weighed him down on the bed.

Theo lowered his gaze. His stomach flip-flopped.

Sometime during the night, Hunter had turned and embraced him.

Theo stared, his pulse fairly thundering as he absorbed it all.

Hunter's eyelashes rested lightly on his cheeks where he slept tucked up against Theo's chest. His strong legs were entwined intimately with Theo's and he'd wrapped his arms snuggly around Theo's body.

Theo swallowed a sigh of happiness.

God, I wish we could stay like this forever.

He slowly relaxed back down on the bed, his heart throbbing with a bittersweet emotion. He knew he was falling fast for the man sleeping next to him. And it wasn't just physical.

In the days since Hunter had started driving him around Twilight Falls, Theo had come to realize that he wasn't just hot and sassy, but smart, kind, and generous to a fault. He was also wickedly funny, quick to defend those he cared for, and fiercely protective of his friends and employees.

It's no wonder I'm losing my heart to him.

Lines wrinkled his brow a moment later.

He suspected there had to be a good reason why Hunter was so afraid to be a bottom. He just hoped the day would soon come when Hunter felt able to talk to him about it.

Hunter murmured something in his sleep. He shifted closer and nuzzled Theo's chest.

Theo sucked in air when Hunter's lips brushed his bare skin.

Hunter stiffened. His eyes snapped open.

He looked up and stared at Theo. "Hmm."

Theo clamped down on his roaring libido and smiled gently at Hunter's endearingly flustered expression. "'Morning."

Color stained Hunter's cheeks when he realized he was clinging wantonly to Theo. He started to disentangle himself from Theo and froze.

Theo muffled a groan. Hunter's thigh had just brushed against his erection.

"I'm sorry. That's just a physiological response."

Hunter blushed fiercely at Theo's mumbled apology. That was when Theo felt something hard nudging his own groin.

Hunter was as aroused as he was.

Theo bit his lower lip and swallowed a chuckle.

"Well, this is a problem," he finally managed in a strangled voice.

Hunter groaned. "I can't believe you're laughing right now."

"It can't be helped," Theo said pragmatically. "We're both guys."

Hunter sighed. "I'll take a shower first." He started to pull away.

Theo tightened his arm around Hunter's waist. "Do you have to?"

Hunter narrowed his eyes at him.

"I mean, there are more…pleasant ways to deal with

this dilemma, don't you think?" Theo murmured suggestively.

"I thought you said you wouldn't do anything I didn't want you to do," Hunter said stiffly.

Theo eyed Hunter steadily and moved his thigh.

Hunter muffled a curse when the motion caused Theo's leg to rub against his erection.

"I think you want this as badly as I do," Theo said huskily.

Hunter's eyes turned stormy gray. His gaze dropped to Theo's mouth.

"Has anyone ever told you you are a bad influence?"

Theo smiled. "Me? Never."

Hunter frowned. "Somehow, I doubt that."

Theo lifted a hand to Hunter's face. "So, what will it be? Cold shower or…something else?" He rubbed his thumb lightly across Hunter's lower lip.

Hunter drew a shallow breath. His eyes darkened.

"No penetrative sex," he warned adamantly.

Theo shook his head, his heart thundering against his ribs. "No penetrative sex."

Hunter stared heatedly at Theo. He parted his lips and slowly sucked Theo's finger into the velvety hotness of his mouth.

Theo cursed.

CHAPTER 18

HUNTER GRINNED BEFORE WRAPPING HIS TONGUE AROUND Theo's thumb. He hollowed his cheeks and moved his head to and fro at a leisurely pace, mimicking a blowjob. Now that he'd come to terms with the fact that this was going to happen, he was determined to enjoy the hell out it.

Theo tolerated a few seconds of the delicious torture Hunter was inflicting on his finger before slipping it out of his mouth. He swooped down and took Hunter's lips in a torrid kiss, his expression feverish with desire.

Hunter groaned and clutched at Theo's shoulders as Theo invaded his mouth with a demanding tongue. He loved it when Theo took over their kissing.

Pleasure hummed through Hunter as Theo frenched him with masterful ease. He arched his back and squirmed, helpless to control the motion of his body as he rubbed himself wantonly against Theo.

They both gasped when the movement kneaded their erections together.

"Your dick feels so hot," Theo mumbled. "I can't wait to take you in my mouth!"

Hunter's cock throbbed at Theo's passionate words.

Theo's eyes were green with longing as he pushed Hunter on his back. Hunter's eyes widened when Theo wrenched his T-shirt up and closed his mouth on Hunter's right nipple.

Hunter grunted, surprised. His hand found Theo's hair. He started to yank Theo away. "Theo, wait. I—"

Theo resisted the motion, circled Hunter's hard nub teasingly with his tongue, and sucked.

Hunter's eyes widened. *"Oh!"*

His shocked cry of pleasure echoed around the bedroom. Hunter would have blushed at the erotic sound had he not fallen under the spell of Theo's mouth where Theo was suckling and kissing and biting his chest. Toe-curling bolts of electricity stabbed through him with Theo's every move and his cock pulsed in tandem with the hungry motion of Theo's hot lips and tongue.

He never would have imagined he'd be a nipple man but Theo was proving him wrong.

Theo growled and switched his attention to Hunter's left pec.

Hunter keened softly as he drowned in the blistering new sensations Theo was eliciting from his body. It was as if Theo knew his erogenous zones better than he knew them himself. He buried his hands in Theo's hair and gave himself over to Theo, trusting he would take them both through safely to the other side of the storm sweeping over them.

Theo raised his head and stared hotly at Hunter, as if

he'd sensed Hunter's silent surrender. He took Hunter's mouth in another kiss full of passion and promise.

Precum oozed out of Hunter's swollen cock and dampened the cotton material of his boxers as he moved restlessly beneath Theo, his vision filling with a red haze of desire as Theo melded their tongues together.

No one had ever made Hunter feel like this before. So hot. So vulnerable. So exposed under another human being's touch and gaze.

And so loved.

He could feel Theo's emotions in the way he was touching him.

Could feel that Theo cherished him as much as he desired him.

Theo kissed Hunter's throat, lavished Hunter's nipples with tender sucks and bites that had him gasping and arching off the bed, and slowly worked his way down Hunter's six-pack and his trembling belly.

Hunter moaned when Theo swirled the inside of his belly button with his tongue and tugged his pajama bottoms and boxers down his hips. His erection sprang free, flushed and wet and straining for release.

"Your dick is so beautiful." Theo's breath tickled Hunter's burning flesh and pubes, drawing a wanton sound from him. "I could suck you for hours."

Hunter lifted his head off the pillow in time to see Theo take him into his mouth.

He cried out and bucked his hips, his orgasm so close he knew it wouldn't take Theo long to bring him to his climax.

Theo grunted and clutched Hunter's hip with his good

hand as he bobbed his head up and down. He hollowed his cheeks and swallowed Hunter's cock all the way to the back of his mouth, his hot lips and tongue relentlessly lashing Hunter's sensitive shaft.

Stars exploded in front of Hunter's eyes when the head of his dick rubbed against the velvety softness of Theo's throat. He clutched at Theo's hair with both hands, incoherent cries and moans escaping his lips.

"Oh Jesus! That feels SO good!"

Hunter twisted his fingers in Theo's hair and dug his heels into the mattress, his hips rolling in an uncontrollable rhythm as he fucked Theo's mouth.

Theo's hand bit into Hunter's thigh when Hunter exploded at the back of his throat a moment later. He breathed heavily through his nose as he gulped and swallowed Hunter's cum with greedy motions of his mouth, fingers moving to gently caress Hunter's twitching balls.

A raspy groan left Hunter when Theo finally released his spent dick.

Theo yanked Hunter's pajama bottoms off his legs and cast them on the floor, his movement frenzied.

Hunter's eyes rounded when Theo flipped him on his side and crowded his back.

"What are you—*oh!*" Hunter gasped when something hard and hot nudged his butt.

"I won't enter you," Theo said huskily in Hunter's right ear. "I just want to feel you!" He slipped his erection down the crack of Hunter's ass and pushed in between his legs.

Blood pounded in Hunter's ears as Theo gripped his right hip and started thrusting his cock through the narrow gap of his thighs.

"Your—your arm!" Hunter stammered when he felt Theo's cast on his waist.

"It's okay!" Theo groaned. "Trust me, the only thing in pain right now is my dick!" He reached around and started fondling Hunter's cock.

Hunter moaned and turned his head, seeking Theo's mouth.

Theo obliged and kissed him passionately.

Hunter's heart thumped violently in his chest as he absorbed the thrilling sensation of Theo's rock hard shaft moving sensuously between his trembling flesh. He bucked his hips and gasped against Theo's lips when Theo worked his other hand under him and started playing with his left nipple, fingers pinching and pulling and twisting the swollen, hardened nub.

Hunter's dick soon swelled and hardened, pleasure swamping him under Theo's tender, erotic ministrations.

Theo's cock rubbed the underside of Hunter's balls and the back of his shaft as he pumped his hips against Hunter's ass, his precum making a sticky mess between Hunter's thighs.

Hunter wrapped one hand around Theo's nape and pulled him closer before reaching down and touching the head of Theo's cock where he was punching through the gap in his legs.

Theo wrenched his mouth from Hunter's. "Fuck!"

"I believe you are!" Hunter panted. "Fucking me. With this!"

Theo groaned when Hunter started rubbing his cock. "I'm not going to last if you keep doing that!"

Hunter rubbed his ass against Theo's groin and thrust

his erection through Theo's fingers. "That's the goal, isn't it?"

Theo hissed. "You little—"

Hunter nipped at Theo's lower lip. "Make me come too."

Theo's eyes blazed a brilliant green. He buried his face in Hunter's neck as he rammed his erection repeatedly in the snug warmth of Hunter's thighs, grunts of pleasure leaving his nose. Hunter moaned and bowed his neck, giving Theo better access. Theo bit down on his flesh, his fingers playing relentlessly with Hunter's body as he brought them closer and closer to an earth-shattering orgasm.

Their hoarse shouts echoed around the room when they climaxed a moment later, the bed creaking under the motions of their thrusting, shuddering bodies, the sheets damp with their sweat and cum.

CHAPTER 19

"What's it like to be a bottom?"

Alex spat out a mouthful of his coffee.

Elijah's eclair splattered on his plate as he dropped his pastry, his jaw sagging open.

Hunter grimaced where he leaned against the countertop. "Sorry."

They were in the kitchen of *La Petite Bouche Gourmande*. A low drone of conversation came through the door from the front of the shop. Even though it was after lunchtime on a Saturday, the place was packed. Elijah was a renowned chef who'd trained and worked in a Michelin star restaurant in Paris, and his store drew scores of people from the nearby towns every weekend.

Alex dabbed at the wet patches on his T-shirt and jeans with the napkin Elijah offered him before frowning at Hunter. "What kind of question is that?"

Hunter tried not to squirm under their stares.

"I'm just curious," he said with a nonchalant shrug.

Ten days had passed since he and Theo slept together

for the first time and had non-penetrative sex. Hunter had spent nearly every night at Theo's place since then, their passion for one another unabated as they pleasured each other with their mouths and hands.

Elijah's expression cleared. "Is this about Theo?"

"Oh." Alex stared at the chef, his surprise plain to see. "You know about Hunter and Theo?"

"Izzy tattled to Carter." Elijah hesitated. "I think Carter knew something was up even before that though."

Hunter muttered something under his breath about meddlesome friends.

Alex narrowed his eyes at Hunter. "Wait. Does this mean you want to bottom for Theo?"

Hunter's cheeks warmed under Alex's shrewd gaze. "What makes you think it's not the other way around?"

Elijah and Alex studied him with dubious expressions.

"The way you guys are looking at me is seriously pissing me off," Hunter said testily.

"To be honest, I always assumed you were a bottom," Elijah murmured.

"Same here," Alex said with a nod.

Hunter scowled. "Well, I'm not."

"But you want to know what it feels like?" Elijah said carefully.

Hunter blew out a sigh.

This was a bad idea.

"Forget about it. I'm gonna go." He put his coffee down.

"Not so fast," Alex said sharply. "It's clear something's bugging you, otherwise you wouldn't have asked such a question of us."

Hunter hesitated where he stood poised to make a run for the door. He fisted his hands and turned to face his friends.

They are the only ones I can talk to about this.

"I—I want to have sex with Theo," Hunter finally admitted in a low voice, his gaze on the floor. He looked up and met Alex and Elijah's eyes defiantly. "But I'm scared. Because of something that happened to me in the past."

Alex's eyes widened. It was the first time Hunter had ever mentioned his fear of bottoming to either of them.

"Have you talked to Theo about this?" Alex said after a while.

"No," Hunter mumbled. "I'm too embarrassed to broach the subject with him."

"I think you should," Alex murmured. "Talk to him."

"To answer your question, I love being a bottom," Elijah admitted quietly in the awkward silence that befell them. "My first few times were painful for sure, but after that, I found it incredibly pleasurable. It helped that both I and my lovers knew how to prepare my body for the act."

"Same," Alex muttered. "I can do both, but I like bottoming more than topping. And Finn likes it too."

Hunter drew a sharp breath. "Wait. You're saying Finn's bottomed for you?!"

"Yeah. And since I'm one too, I made sure his first time was great." Alex scratched his cheek. "Not to blow my own trumpet, but he's kind of addicted to it."

Hunter's heart thumped against his ribs as he stared at Alex.

Elijah rubbed his chin thoughtfully. "So, is it tips you're after?"

~

THEO OPENED HIS FRONT DOOR ON SUNDAY MORNING AND found Hunter sitting on his porch. A smile curved his lips.

"Hey. This is a nice surprise."

Hunter rose and turned to face him, his expression strangely serious.

"I know we didn't make plans for today, but are you free right now? I want to take you somewhere."

Surprise darted through Theo at Hunter's solemn request.

"Sure. I was coming over to see if you wanted to go for a walk anyway."

Hunter waited patiently while Theo grabbed a jacket. They walked over to his Jeep and were soon on their way out of their estate.

Hunter drove north, into the mountains that surrounded Twilight Falls. Shadows engulfed them as they entered the forest, sunlight dancing through the trees to dapple them with patches of light.

Theo's gaze fell on Hunter's strong, tanned fingers where his hands rested on the steering wheel.

The memory of the last time they'd made love two nights ago flashed before his eyes. Hunter had straddled him and rubbed their erections together with one hand while he undulated his hips seductively above Theo's groin, his other hand entwined tightly with Theo's where he pressed it in the bed, his heated eyes locked on

Theo's while he groaned and panted in pleasure above him.

Theo's cock throbbed at the vivid recollection. He shifted slightly in his seat and focused his attention on the scenery outside the vehicle. Light sparkled off water at the bottom of the valley to his right.

Hunter slowed and turned into a side road that wound its way down the mountain. Theo's eyes widened when he saw a sign through the trees a quarter mile later. It said "Sunrise Care Home."

The road became a driveway.

Twilight Falls River finally appeared around a bend in the land.

A large, rambling, pretty two-story building with a red-shingle roof straddled a gentle slope on the left.

Hunter pulled into the parking lot outside the establishment and turned the Jeep's engine off. He unclipped his belt, twisted around, and grabbed something from the back seat.

Theo stared at the beautiful bouquet of camellias in Hunter's hand.

Hunter's expression softened as he met Theo's puzzled gaze.

"What are we doing here?" Theo asked quietly.

"Visiting a friend," Hunter replied. "I want to introduce you to him."

Theo's heart pounded dully against his ribs as he followed Hunter out of the vehicle and up the steps to the terrace that wrapped around the care home.

He couldn't shake the feeling that Hunter bringing him here was something incredibly special.

They entered a brightly-lit foyer and headed over to a reception desk.

A brunette in a white uniform was bent over a computer behind the counter. She looked up at their steps, a polite smile on her face. Her expression brightened when she spotted Hunter, her face relaxing in a genuine beam.

"Hey, hot stuff."

"Hi, Lisa," Hunter greeted.

The brunette's gaze shifted to Theo. Appreciation dawned in her eyes. "Who's the stud?"

Hunter sighed. "This is Theo Miller. He's…a friend. Theo, this is Lisa."

Theo stilled, not sure whether it was surprise or disappointment he felt at Hunter's description of their relationship.

Lisa arched an eyebrow, her shrewd expression telling Theo she hadn't missed his reaction.

"Hi, Theo." She stared from Theo to Hunter. "You sure he's just a friend? 'Cause I'm getting all kinds of vibes looking at the two of you. And by vibes, I mean sexy stuff."

Theo smiled at her brazen declaration.

Hunter scowled. "That's none of your business. Now, please stop fantasizing about whatever it is you're imagining right now and give me the damn visitor's log."

Lisa rolled her eyes. "Wow, touchy much?" She passed the book to him.

From their exchange, Theo gathered they were close friends.

Hunter signed them in. He started to hand the visitor's

log back and paused, his gaze above the line where he'd just scribbled their names.

"Oh. Did I miss Elaine?"

"Yup. She left twenty minutes ago." Lisa cocked her head at the bouquet in Hunter's hand. "I see you brought his favorite flowers."

Hunter glanced at the camellias. A tender smile lit his face. "He really does love these, doesn't he?"

Something that felt a lot like jealousy pierced Theo's chest then. He masked the ugly emotion behind a neutral expression and followed Hunter as he headed down a passage to the left of the reception.

CHAPTER 20

THEY HEADED UP TO THE SECOND FLOOR AND NAVIGATED A series of pleasantly decorated corridors. Whoever was in charge of the care home kept it immaculate. Theo could tell the same attention was given to the residents who lived there from the glimpses he caught of the rooms they passed.

They came to a door at the far end of the building.

Hunter knocked lightly. "I'm coming in." He opened the door.

Theo's first impression of the room they entered was of space and light.

Pretty curtains fluttered lightly in a gentle breeze wafting through the dual aspect windows framing enchanting views of the forest and the river.

Lying on a medical bed in the middle of the gaily painted room was a man attached to an IV drip. His long eyelashes rested against his cheeks, his handsome face relaxed as he slept. He was freshly-shaven and his dark locks curled slightly at his nape.

"Hi, Miles," Hunter said quietly.

He walked over to the dresser by the bed, swapped the limp flowers in one of the vases with the fresh camellias, and leaned down to brush his lips against the man's forehead.

"You look good, buddy." Hunter grimaced slightly. "Sorry I haven't visited lately." He turned and beckoned Theo over.

Theo approached the bed, his pulse racing.

"Miles, this is Theo," Hunter told the sleeping man. "Theo, this is Miles Martinez."

"It's a pleasure to meet you, Miles," Theo said softly.

Hunter sat on the edge of the bed and took Miles's hand in his own. He started talking quietly to the unconscious man, telling him everything he'd been up to in the last couple of weeks, minus the hot sex.

Theo brought a chair over and sat silently by Hunter's side. Though he didn't know the reason why Miles Martinez was in a care home, he could tell from the sad light in Hunter's eyes that the story was a painful one.

Hunter went on to narrate amusing incidents the rest of his circle of friends had been involved in, including how badly Tristan had thrashed them at their weekly poker games. His voice lightened and his face loosened up the more he talked.

Theo couldn't help but feel that for Hunter, this was some kind of cathartic experience. He could tell from the vases of flowers dotted around the room that Miles Martinez's friends visited him regularly and wondered if all of them did this too.

They bade their goodbyes to the sleeping man an hour later.

To Theo's surprise, Hunter led him to a visitor's room on the first floor. They made themselves coffee in the kitchen area and headed out onto the terrace fronting the river. Theo followed Hunter as he strolled down the steps and wandered into the garden.

Hunter stopped and sat down on a bench overlooking the river.

Theo took the spot next to him.

"It was shortly after my eighteen birthday that the accident happened," Hunter finally said after a long silence. "It was the fourth of July. We'd gone up the mountain to our favorite picnic spot to watch the fireworks, like we'd done for a couple of years. We were coming back to Twilight Falls when a drunk driver on the other side of the road crossed the center line. Alex was behind the wheel." He paused, a muscle twitching in his jawline. "Were it not for Alex's reflexes that day, the accident would have been much worse. We crashed in the trees on the side of the road instead of going over the side of the mountain. Six of us walked out of Alex's mom's truck that night, with only a handful of scratches and bruises between us." His voice grew husky. "Miles didn't. He fell into a coma and hasn't woken up since."

Theo reached across and clasped Hunter's hand. "I'm so sorry."

Hunter swallowed convulsively, his eyes shimmering with a trace of wetness. "Thank you."

Theo's heart clenched with a wave of pain as he recalled Hunter's friends' smiling faces. Having witnessed how close they were, he knew Miles's condition had to weigh heavily on all of their consciences.

No wonder they're so protective of one another.

"Miles's mom never held Alex or any of us responsible for the accident. Alex was devastated." Hunter stared into the distance. "He left Twilight Falls a short time after the accident. I don't think he actually forgave himself until he came back and met Finn this year."

"What do the doctors say?" Theo asked after a while. "About Miles's chances?"

Hunter's fingers clenched around Theo's. "They think there's still hope. That Miles might wake up one day and be okay. But I—" He stopped and faltered. "I just don't know. It breaks my heart every time I see him lying in that bed," he whispered, his voice trembling.

Theo pulled Hunter close and pressed a loving kiss to his temple. Hunter stiffened slightly before relaxing in his embrace. The roar of the river echoed across the valley in the lull that followed.

"Six months after the accident, we went to this bar in the next town. It was just Tristan, Drake, Wyatt, and me. It was the first time we'd gone out since the accident. I got rip roaring drunk and went to the motel across the road with this guy I hooked up with."

Theo held his breath. He could feel Hunter's heart thundering where he held him.

"That was the first time I bottomed for someone," Hunter continued. "We were so buzzed we didn't realize how much damage he'd caused until we woke up a few hours later. Tristan was livid. He'd stayed back looking for me and had left some twenty voicemails on my phone.

The guy I was with panicked when he saw all the blood and called an ambulance. Tristan was still outside the bar when they turned up. I don't think I ever saw him go as white in his entire life as he did when he saw the bedsheet."

Theo swallowed the hard lump in his throat, anger and agony storming through him in equal measures. He tightened his hold on Hunter.

"That was the night my dad found out I was gay," Hunter continued softly. "I gotta say, my old man took it in stride like a trooper. He lectured me big time afterward but, that night, he was just my dad. He told me he'd suspected I was batting for the other team for some time, considering my lack of girlfriends." He paused. "I was in the hospital for a week."

Theo closed his eyes briefly.

"Dammit Hunter," he ground out in a frustrated voice.

"Yeah, well, you're not the only one who said that," Hunter muttered. "Tristan was like a hawk after that incident. I swear he wanted to be in the room the next time I had sex. Luckily, I was in college by then. I never got that drunk again. And I always insisted on being a top."

Theo took a shaky breath. He disentangled himself from Hunter, twisted on the bench, and cradled Hunter's chin in his hand.

"It's okay. I want to be with you. Sex isn't important."

As he looked into the beautiful gray eyes opposite him, Theo knew he meant every word he'd just said. Just as he knew that he'd fallen completely and utterly in love with the bewitching man who sat looking at him with an enigmatic expression.

Hunter closed his fingers over Theo's hand and turned his face to press a kiss in Theo's palm, the look in his eyes telling Theo he knew what those words meant.

"Thank you for saying that," he breathed. "But sex matters to me. And I know it matters to you. The reason I brought you here and told you that story is because I want to try again."

Theo blinked, not sure he'd heard correctly. "What?"

Hunter's eyes darkened. "I want to have sex with you, Theo. Real sex. As in, I want to go all the way."

Theo's heart drummed rapidly in his chest as he stared at Hunter.

"Are you—are you sure?" he stammered. "We don't have—"

Hunter narrowed his eyes. "I made up my mind. We are doing this, Miller."

Theo choked on his breath. He burst out laughing in the next instant.

Hunter watched him as if he'd gone crazy.

"I'm sorry!" Theo said between chuckles. "It's just—I've never seen anyone so determined to jump my bones before."

Hunter flushed a delicate shade of pink.

"Well, you have lovely bones," he grumbled, his ears flaming.

CHAPTER 21

HUNTER TURNED THE SHOWER OFF AND STEPPED OUT ONTO the soft weaved mat. He could feel his heart racing wildly in his chest as he dried himself with one of Theo's bath towels. Theo's body wash enveloped him in a delicious cloud of evergreens, so much so he felt as if he was already in Theo's arms. And it was driving him crazy.

Hunter dropped a hand to his swelling arousal and stared at the bathroom door.

Theo was waiting for him on the other side.

Hunter hesitated before sliding a hand down his back and over his butt cheeks. He slipped a finger inside his crack and found his pucker. He shivered as he played with his softened folds.

He'd cleaned himself thoroughly in preparation for what he and Theo were about to do and had been pleasantly shocked by how easily he'd been able to slip a finger inside his back passage once he'd followed the instructions Alex and Elijah had given him on how to get his body ready for penetration. Though he'd done this plenty of times for the guys he'd topped, Hunter had always balked at the thought of having it done to him.

He wrapped the towel around his waist, took a deep breath, and headed determinedly out into the bedroom.

Theo was sitting naked in the middle of the bed, a pensive expression on his face and his cast a sharp contrast against his tanned skin.

Hunter's mind went blank. Though he'd seen Theo naked plenty of times before, every time felt like the first all over again.

Theo's body was all hard angles and toned muscles. His broad shoulders tapered down to impressive pecs and a well-defined six-pack that gave way to narrow hips, a generously endowed cock and balls, and strong, long legs.

Goosebumps broke out across Hunter's skin as he stared at Theo's dick. The thought of having Theo's thick member buried deep inside his body enthralled and scared him in equal measure.

Yet, Hunter knew he needed to do this. *Wanted* to do this.

The contents of the bag he'd brought with him was scattered in front of Theo. Heat warmed Hunter's cheeks as he gazed at the range of anal beads and butt plugs spread out before Theo. There were a couple of bottles of scented lube and boxes of condoms too.

"When exactly did you get these?" Theo lifted a slim, vibrating butt plug and examined it critically from every possible angle.

"I ordered them online a few days ago," Hunter confessed.

Theo stared at him, nonplussed. "You've been thinking about it that long?"

Hunter hesitated before dipping his chin.

Theo's eyes darkened. He held out a hand to Hunter. "Come here."

Theo's husky voice made Hunter's cock throb. He obeyed Theo's command and climbed on the bed, feeling strangely self-conscious all of a sudden. Theo tugged the towel off his hips and dropped it on the floor.

Hunter shuddered when Theo trailed light fingers down his tense belly to his trembling erection. Theo leaned in and nibbled on Hunter's right earlobe.

"Why don't we try my fingers first?" he whispered in Hunter's ear.

Hunter blushed fiercely and swallowed before nodding jerkily. He was so turned on it was a miracle he hadn't exploded at the first touch of Theo's hand.

Theo kissed him then, his mouth hot and hungry.

Hunter melted against him, his senses fairly drowning with desire. He moaned when Theo probed his lips with his tongue while pinching and twisting his nipples with his clever fingers.

"Theo!" Hunter gasped. He locked his arms demandingly around Theo's neck.

Theo smiled as his silent plea. He dipped his head, closed his teeth on Hunter's right nipple, and tugged gently.

"*Ah!*" Hunter arched his back and closed his eyes tight, his cock pulsing precum at the sharp pleasure-pain of the sting. He pushed his chest toward Theo's mouth.

Theo alternated between kissing and biting Hunter's

hardened nubs, every pull and suck sending the sweetest spasm through Hunter's back passage. He ran his hand tantalizing across Hunter's six-pack and belly, touching and exploring his hot flesh.

"Theo?" Hunter breathed.

"Yes, Hunter?" Theo mumbled against Hunter's left pec.

Hunter rocked his hips and nudged his dick against Theo's thigh.

"Touch me," Hunter pleaded softly.

A feral light flashed in Theo's eyes. His hand found Hunter's cock again. He started teasing and stroking him, his lips and teeth sucking and nibbling Hunter's throat.

Hunter cursed, straddled Theo's hips, and reached down.

Theo hissed when Hunter closed his hand on his straining erection.

"Shit!" he mumbled, his gaze dark with passion. "That feels good! Don't stop!"

Hunter groaned, his hips rolling instinctively against Theo's groin as they stroked one another.

Theo grabbed a condom, ripped the foil with his teeth, and rolled the rubber over his left index finger. He flipped a bottle of lube open and coated the condom liberally with the scented liquid.

Hunter stiffened when Theo slipped his good hand around his back and gently kneaded his right butt cheek.

"Relax," Theo murmured in Hunter's ear. "Just feel me." He reached down with his injured arm and started rubbing Hunter's cock again.

Hunter concentrated on the wicked feel of Theo's

fingers on his hard flesh and moved his own hand on Theo's erection. A startled yelp escaped him when Theo dipped a cool finger inside his crack and caressed his opening.

Theo stilled. "Do you want me to stop?"

Hunter hugged Theo's shoulders tightly and buried his face in Theo's neck.

"No," he whispered tremulously.

Theo kissed his hair. "Tell you what," he murmured lovingly. "Why don't we try something different?"

Surprise jolted Hunter when Theo settled onto his back. He directed Hunter to crawl upside down on top of him.

Hunter's heart thudded wildly when he found himself face to face with Theo's raging erection. He'd never made love in this position before. He pressed his mouth tentatively against Theo's shaft before trailing a teasing tongue up his hard length.

He was rewarded by a loud curse.

A shiver shot down Hunter's spine when Theo's hot breath washed across his ass and balls. Theo's hand found Hunter's straining cock and directed it past his hungry lips.

CHAPTER 22

HUNTER GASPED, HIS EYES SLAMMING WIDE OPEN AT THE wicked feeling of Theo swallowing him whole. The angle at which he was penetrating Theo's mouth felt different and new and oh-so-fucking hot. He moaned when Theo raised and lowered his head rhythmically off the pillow and started blowing him, the sounds his lips and tongue made on Hunter's aching flesh so arousing it was a miracle he hadn't exploded yet.

Theo thrust his hips demandingly toward Hunter's face.

Hunter obliged and took the head of Theo's dick inside his mouth. Theo's musky precum hit his tongue. Lust stormed Hunter at the intoxicating, salty taste. He swirled his tongue languidly around the tip of Theo's cock and was rewarded with another loud curse when Theo shuddered and bucked against his palate.

Hunter wrapped one hand around the base of Theo's stiff cock and started working him hard and deep, his cheeks bulging as he swallowed Theo's quivering shaft all the way to the back of his throat.

An animal sound left Theo where he was blowing Hunter's dick.

Hunter shivered as Theo's breath tickled his erection. He moaned when Theo suddenly let go of his cock, hungry for more.

Strong fingers parted his butt cheeks.

Hunter gasped when Theo's heated breath brushed across his hole. His opening twitched and contracted.

"Theo, wait! You can't—"

"So pretty," Theo said huskily, ignoring Hunter's protest. "Your ass is beautiful."

Hunter cried out when Theo kissed his pucker. *"Oh!"*

Electric tingles shot through his body from where Theo was delivering his ardent ministrations, his wet lips rubbing and sucking sweetly on Hunter's softened folds.

"Theo!" Hunter reached back and curled a hand in Theo's hair, not sure whether he wanted to push him away or pull him in.

Theo paused. "Want me to stop?"

Theo's low growl made Hunter shiver.

It was hungry and possessive and was pushing all of Hunter's buttons perfectly.

White light exploded in front of Hunter's eyes in the next instant.

Theo had flicking the tip of his stiff tongue across Hunter's entrance and was circling his rim in lazy, heady swirls that made his vision go hazy.

"Jesus!" Hunter's fingers clenched spasmodically in Theo's locks.

"I'm going to take that as no," Theo grunted.

He furrowed his tongue and poked the end inside Hunter's opening.

Hunter's eyes rounded.

A guttural sound left him as Theo stabbed his quivering pucker repeatedly with his tongue, slowly stretching him open and making him wet.

Hunter shuddered as he melted from the new, wicked sensations Theo was eliciting from his body.

An ache started deep inside him. One he'd never felt before. He started rocked his hips against Theo's face, begging for something. Something he couldn't fathom. His entire body went rigid when Theo removed his tongue and slipped a lubed-up finger inside him.

Hunter cried out and came violently, his cock pulsing out a powerful jet of precum on Theo's chest and belly.

Theo's heart thumped against his ribs as Hunter trembled and shuddered above him, his hole spasming hungrily around Theo's index finger while his balls contracted in pleasure and his dick spurted out a thick stream of musky essence. He couldn't believe how sensitive Hunter was or how quickly he'd climaxed from having his ass played with.

Theo's cock throbbed painfully between his thighs. Though he hadn't found his own release yet, he knew it was too soon for him to enter Hunter.

One thing had become inherently clear though.

Hunter was a natural born bottom and would find anal sex highly enjoyable.

Hunter gasped when Theo slipped his finger out of his hole until only the tip stretched his opening. His folds quivered and gripped Theo's condom-covered flesh.

Theo opened his mouth and sank his teeth gently in Hunter's left butt cheek at the same time he pushed back in.

Hunter's low moan of pleasure made Theo's blood sing with desire.

Now that he knew how receptive Hunter's body was to penetration, he was determined to get him ready for the ultimate act of sex. He cursed when Hunter's hand and mouth found his painfully stiff erection once more.

The hungry sound Hunter made as he started blowing Theo almost made Theo come there and then.

Hunter started rolling his hips demandingly against Theo's hand, his flushed dick swelling with fresh arousal where he rubbed it against Theo's pecs.

Theo's belly clenched when he met Hunter's upside down gaze where Hunter looked down the length of their bodies at him.

"More!" Hunter panted, his gray eyes glazed with passion. "I want to feel you more!"

Theo gnashed his teeth and gave Hunter exactly what he was begging for, thrusting and twisting his finger in and out of Hunter's eager ass.

A shout left Hunter when Theo found his prostate. Theo hissed as Hunter squeezed his finger in a vise-like grip, sucking him in even deeper.

"Oh God!" Hunter moaned. "That feels—*fuck!*"

A grunt left Theo when Hunter clenched his hand painfully around the base of Theo's rock hard shaft. Theo slipped his finger out of Hunter, inserted his middle digit inside the condom, grabbed the bottle of lube, and poured the cool liquid directly on Hunter's loosening hole.

Hunter's breath caught when Theo carefully pushed his two fingers inside his back passage.

"Ah!"

He arched his back and shivered deliciously, his hips rocking against Theo's hand, his body swallowing Theo's fingers to the knuckles and gripping ever so tightly, as if he never wanted to let go.

It took all of Theo's willpower not to flip Hunter on his back, spread Hunter's thighs, and thrust his raging erection repeatedly inside Hunter's body to find his much needed release.

The way Hunter was gasping and moaning and grasping Theo's fingers with his hungry hole told Theo he was close to climaxing again.

Theo reached down clumsily with his injured arm and guided his engorged cock blindly to Hunter's mouth.

Hunter obeyed his command and started sucking him again.

Theo dug his heels in the bed and punched his hips up, his orgasm tightening his body while he continued stretching and fucking Hunter's back passage with his slicked up fingers. His movements grew more uncontrolled as he neared his climax.

Hunter responded in equal measure, his hips rocking wildly against Theo's good hand, his head bobbing jerkily up and down Theo's inflamed cock, taking him all the way into the velvety depths of his hungry throat.

A white haze filled Theo's vision. He came with a loud shout, his spine bowing powerfully off the bed. His cock throbbed with the most insane pleasure as he pumped his hot seed deep inside Hunter's famished mouth. Hunter's muffled cries shuddered around Theo's twitching cock as he too crested his climax, his cock shooting cum onto Theo's chest and belly, his back passage pulsing enticingly around Theo's fingers.

CHAPTER 23

"HELLO? EARTH TO HUNTER?"

Hunter blinked away the torrid images playing across his mind's eye and looked at Imogen distractedly over his cup of coffee. "What?"

"We need to order some more of those walking boots that came in last month." Imogen stared. "You have the strangest expression on your face."

Hunter tried his damnedest not to flush. He couldn't believe he'd been caught daydreaming about making love with Theo. He stilled at that thought. He could no longer deny what was happening between him and Theo. Not after Sunday night.

He was falling in love and hard.

"Are you blushing?" Imogen muttered.

Hunter silently cursed himself. "No. And the answer is yes to placing that order."

He walked out of the staff kitchen under Imogen's suspicious gaze, checked that Benji and Chloe were okay in the front store, and headed into the back office. His cell phone buzzed just as he sat behind his desk. It was Theo.

Theo: Wanna grab some lunch?

Hunter's pulse jumped. He tapped out a reply.

Hunter: Sure.

Theo: One o'clock? Come over to the shop. I have a surprise for you.

Hunter told himself he wasn't counting down the minutes to his impromptu lunch date with Theo when he relieved Benji and Chloe at the till. He left Imogen behind the counter a short while later and headed across the road dead on the hour.

Codie finished serving a customer just as Hunter entered *Miller*. He greeted him with a smile before pointing to a room at the end of the corridor behind him.

"Theo's in there."

Hunter nodded and headed down the hallway. He'd never been inside Theo's office before and was curious as to what it looked like. He was also eager to find out exactly what Theo had in store for him.

Hunter stopped outside the door and hesitated before knocking, his palms suddenly damp. He felt giddy and nervous all at once, as if he were a teenager falling in love for the first time.

"Come in."

Theo's voice made Hunter's pulse flutter. He took a shallow breath, told himself to calm down, and entered the office.

The room was bigger and brighter than his own workspace at the rear of *Go Thomson!* He scanned the minimalistic design and bare white walls with mild surprise before locking eyes with the man he was looking for.

Theo was sitting on a couch to the left. Spread out on the coffee table before him were sandwiches, a plate of deli meats, and drinks.

"I thought we could have a picnic." Theo grinned at Hunter's startled stare.

Hunter's chest twisted with a flurry of emotions. It was scary how warm and cherished Theo's smile made him feel. He masked his reaction behind a wry expression and walked over to the couch.

"This place feels kinda...empty."

Theo chuckled. "Blame Kate. She designed it like our office in L.A. Come back in a year and I'm sure it'll be different. Codie is a born hoarder." He pointed out the desk crammed with knickknacks at the other end of the room.

A dull ache stabbed through Hunter at Theo's words. He was conscious Theo had only planned to be in Twilight Falls for a couple of months. They were already more than halfway through that time line and neither of them had broached the subject of the future yet.

Something that felt a lot like fear shot through Hunter then.

Does he even want a future with me?

"Hunter?" Faint lines wrinkled Theo's brow. "What's wrong?"

Hunter blinked. "Nothing," he lied. "Let's eat."

They chatted comfortably over lunch, Hunter doing his best to steer away from the thorny topic now at the forefront of his mind. Theo cleared the table after they'd finished and brought fresh coffee over from the kitchen.

"I should get back," Hunter said reluctantly after they finished their drinks.

Theo caressed Hunter's hand lightly where it lay on the couch between them. "Wanna come over tonight?"

Goosebumps broke out across Hunter's skin where Theo was touching him. His cheeks warmed under Theo's sultry gaze.

He couldn't have refused Theo even if he'd wanted to.

"Sure."

"Good." Theo rose and walked over to the door. "There's something I've been meaning to try out. Now's the perfect time to do it." The sound of the lock turning echoed across the room like a gunshot.

"Theo?" Hunter mumbled.

A predatory smile curved Theo's lips. Hunter's heart stuttered.

"Wait right there," Theo ordered. He crossed the floor to his desk, opened a drawer, and took a couple of items out of a bag.

Hunter stared at the thick, black anal beads and the packet of lube Theo had just removed from his desk. He swallowed hard.

He didn't have to be a genius to figure out what it was Theo intended to do with the sex toy he was holding in his hand.

Hunter's dick stirred and his ass throbbed in anticipation of the dirty, titillating act Theo was about to perform on him.

"Take your pants off, Hunter," Theo commanded silkily.

Hunter glanced at the door, the thrill of their illicit deed sending a flood of heat to his face.

I can't believe he really wants to do this right here, right now!

"Codie won't disturb us." Theo came over slowly, his pace steady and measured.

Hunter's breathing accelerated when Theo knelt in front of him.

Theo spread Hunter's thighs wide open and ran a hot hand up his thigh to his belt buckle. "Now, strip."

Theo's masterful voice made Hunter tremble. Theo was in full control of this situation and he wanted Hunter to know it.

Hunter's chest heaved with excitement as he held Theo's stare. He undid his jeans with shaking fingers, slipped them down his legs along with his boxers, and dropped them in a pile next to Theo along with his T-shirt. The leather couch was warm against his bare skin as he sat still and fairly breathless in front of Theo.

"Good." Theo's heated gazed skimmed Hunter's exposed belly and his swelling cock.

There was no way Hunter could hide his growing erection.

A hiss of pleasure left him as Theo stroked a finger from the root of his stiff shaft all the way to the flushed, wet tip.

Theo leaned down and circled the head of Hunter's dick teasingly with his tongue.

Hunter stifled a cry of pleasure behind his hand.

"Put your legs on my shoulders," Theo growled. He opened his mouth and scraped Hunter's engorged flesh lightly with his teeth, drawing another muffled shout from him. "I want to see that cute ass of yours."

Hunter obeyed Theo's thick command dazedly, blood pounding in his ears and drowning out his heavy pants. Cool air caressed the underside of his balls and his taint as he tilted his hips and exposed his most vulnerable part to Theo's hungry gaze.

He shuddered and closed his eyes when Theo ran a thumb over his pucker.

"Damn!"

A low groan escaped Theo at Hunter's throaty gasp. The sound of the packet of lube being ripped open reached Hunter dimly.

Theo's warm, wet fingers were all over him in the next instant.

Hunter chewed his lip and keened softly as Theo rubbed and teased the folds guarding his entrance, bolts of electricity tingling through his back passage. It didn't take long for him to relax and open up to Theo's probing touch.

Theo slipped his thumb inside Hunter as the same time that he swallowed Hunter's cock inside his mouth.

Hunter dug his heels in Theo's back and let out a low, lustful sound. He arched his butt off the couch, driving the head of his shaft all the way to the back of Theo's throat.

Theo grunted and opened his mouth wider to accommodate Hunter. He thrust his thumb slickly in and out of Hunter's ass and bobbed his head on Hunter's quivering erection, his lips and tongue working him skillfully toward a mind-blowing orgasm.

Pleasure sent red waves pulsing across Hunter's vision when Theo drove a second finger in his ass. He hissed when Theo slowly brought a third finger into play, the ring of muscles guarding his back passage stretching tightly to accommodate Theo's invading digits.

Theo stopped his gentle thrusts and lifted his head from Hunter's cock. "Does it hurt?"

Sweat beaded Hunter's upper lip as he opened his eyes and looked down into Theo's concerned gaze.

"No," he mumbled shakily. "It feels…great." He squeezed his hole tentatively around Theo's fingers and shivered when Theo cursed. "Fill me up more!"

A savage groan left Theo at Hunter's husky plea.

He took Hunter's dick in his mouth and plundered his ass with his strong fingers as he blew and deep throated him.

A buzzing noise filled Hunter's world when he climaxed. He curled the fingers of one hand in Theo's hair and bit down hard on the other while he convulsed on the couch, his ass rubbing the leather and his cock pulsing out cum deep inside Theo's throat. Theo gulped and swallowed greedily, his low hums of satisfaction vibrating tantalizingly through Hunter's jerking shaft.

Hunter was still shuddering with pleasure when Theo slipped his fingers out of his hole. Something else replaced them. Something just as thick and warm and wet.

Hunter gasped and looked down in time to see Theo push the first bead all the way inside him.

"Theo!"

A feral expression burned in Theo's eyes as he slipped the second, then the third bead in. Hunter couldn't believe how easily the stout rubber balls were entering his body. A hot sensation throbbed through his back passage as the sex toy slowly filled him to the brim. One of the beads nudged his prostate.

"Oh God!" Hunter moaned, shuddering all over again at the exquisite sensation.

Theo rose on his knees and kissed Hunter passionately while he wedged the final ball through his pucker. Hunter moaned, the musky taste of his cum on Theo's tongue causing his spent dick to twitch.

"I want you to keep this inside you for the rest of the day," Theo murmured against Hunter's mouth. He gave a playful tug on the handle of the sex toy where it rested snuggly against Hunter's taint and swallowed Hunter's hoarse cry.

Hunter's heart thundered in his chest as he gazed into Theo's feverish eyes.

Theo bit down on Hunter's lower lip with his strong, white teeth and tugged gently before sucking the small wound.

"Will you do that for me, Hunter?"

Hunter nodded jerkily, so excited he thought he'd pass out.

"Good," Theo murmured. "The only one allowed to take that out of you is me." He rose to his feet, unzipped his pants, and guided his weeping erection commandingly to Hunter's mouth. "Now, suck me."

Hunter groaned and closed a hand eagerly around

Theo's cock before parting his lips and taking Theo inside. He dropped his other hand to his stirring arousal and gave himself a hand job while he blew Theo, his ass squeezing the toy nestled snugly inside him.

Hunter spent the afternoon in a state of heightened expectation, his cock twitching whenever one of the beads moved inside him. By the time he drove Theo home and stumbled inside Theo's foyer, he was so close to coming he knew a simple touch would make him explode.

And explode he did when Theo stripped him, dragged him into the shower, and slowly pulled the beads out of his hole, his orgasm so powerful he almost fainted from the incredible pleasure storming his body.

CHAPTER 24

A BUZZING SOUND REACHED THEO THROUGH A FOG OF sleep. He rolled over, grabbed his cell from the nightstand, and blinked fuzzily at the screen.

Kate's number glowed on the display.

Theo checked the time, puzzled. It was barely six in the morning.

He took the call. "Hey. What's up?"

"Sorry to wake you so early," Kate mumbled at the other end of the line. "I had an accident last night."

Theo sat up abruptly, sleep fleeing as effectively as if he'd been drenched with a bucket of cold water. "What?!" Alarm twisted his stomach. "Are you alright?!"

Hunter stirred and mumbled something in his sleep before burrowing his face in Theo's pillow. Theo's heart warmed with affection as he glanced at the man beside him, momentarily distracted.

"Give me a minute." He slipped quietly out of bed, padded barefoot out of the room, and crossed the landing to the glass wall framing the lightening sky at the end of the corridor. "Where are you? What happened?"

"I just got discharged from the ER. I was driving home from a party and a deer ran across the road in front of me. I swerved to avoid him and smashed into a lamp post."

Theo's hand tightened on the phone. "Are you hurt bad? What did the doctors say?"

"I've got plenty of bruises and some pain in my neck, but they don't think it's anything serious. I'm gonna be stiff for a while. And the car's a total write-off."

Warm arms wrapped around Theo's waist from behind.

He looked over his shoulder into Hunter's sleepy face.

"Everything okay?" Hunter mouthed.

"No," Theo mumbled. "Kate had an accident."

Hunter's eyes widened.

"Theo?" Kate asked, puzzled.

"Sorry, Hunter's with me."

Silence rose at the other end of the line.

"Oh," Kate said in a startled voice. "I, er, didn't realize you two were seeing each other."

Theo twisted on his heels and pressed his lips to Hunter's forehead, grateful for his presence. "We are. Very much so. I just haven't had time to tell you."

Hunter flushed at his heartfelt words.

"We need to figure out a plan of action," Theo told Kate.

An uneasy emotion swirled inside Hunter as he watched Theo pack an overnight bag.

"You sure you don't want me to drive you to L.A.?" he said, keeping his tone deliberately light.

Theo shook his head. "Nah. One of our employees is bringing some stock over to the store here. She'll give me a lift back."

They headed downstairs and out of Theo's home.

"How long do you think you'll have to stay away?" Hunter said as they climbed inside his Jeep. He started the engine and headed toward town, his hands stiff where he held the steering wheel.

"A week, maybe," Theo replied. "I'll know more after I see Kate."

Hunter startled slightly when Theo laid a hand on his thigh.

"Just so you know, I'm not happy about this either," Theo said softly. "I don't want to leave you."

Hunter swallowed, no longer surprised that Theo could read him so easily. "It can't be helped."

"No, it can't," Theo murmured. "But it still sucks."

Codie was waiting anxiously on the curb when Hunter pulled up outside *Miller* minutes later.

"I'll come say goodbye." Theo pressed a warm kiss to Hunter's mouth and stepped out of the vehicle.

Hunter watched Theo guide Codie inside the store, still troubled. He parked his Jeep and headed reluctantly toward *Go Thomson!*

Imogen poked her head around the office door a moment later.

"'Morning," she greeted cheerfully. "Want some coffee?

I just made a fresh pot"

"Sure," Hunter mumbled distractedly.

Imogen paused, her smile slipping. "What's wrong?"

Hunter hesitated before telling her about Kate's phone call.

Imogen's eyes widened in horror as she listened. "Gosh! That's terrible! Is she going to be okay?"

"I think so. Theo said she had bruises and was going to be stiff for a while."

Guilt stabbed through Hunter. He knew it was selfish of him to be feeling this way but he couldn't help it. It scared him how attached he'd grown to Theo in the short time they'd spent together and how desperately he didn't want to see him leave.

Theo was true to his word and wandered over to *Go Thomson!* an hour later.

"I'll give you two a moment." Imogen left the office and closed the door quietly in her wake.

Theo and Hunter gazed silently at each other across the room.

"Come here," Theo said softly. He held his good arm out to Hunter.

Hunter rose to his feet and walked slowly around his desk. He closed the distance to Theo and wrapped his arms tightly around Theo's body, stunned by the emotions bubbling through him.

"God, I'm going to miss this," Theo whispered in Hunter's hair.

Hunter buried his face in Theo's chest and listened to Theo's strong heartbeat.

"Don't be a stranger," he mumbled huskily.

Theo pulled back slightly and tipped Hunter's chin with his fingers. His eyes shone brightly as he lowered his head and took Hunter's mouth in a slow kiss full of promise.

"I won't," he murmured hotly against Hunter's lips.

Theo left Twilight Falls a short while later.

Hunter spent the rest of the day in a funk as he waited anxiously for Theo to call him. His cell rang just as he was closing up that evening.

"Hey," Hunter said breathlessly. He swallowed a curse as he almost dropped his phone and juggled the front door keys of *Go Thomson!* with his free hand. "How are things?"

"Not too bad." Theo sighed heavily. "Kate made light of her injuries. She's pretty banged up. I don't think she's going to be able to work for a couple of weeks at least."

Hunter's stomach sank at this news. "Are you staying in L.A. until she comes back?"

"Yeah, I'll have to," Theo muttered. "I'll call you tomorrow and let you know how things are going."

Hunter stared at his cell after Theo ended the call, his stomach a jumble of confusion. He no longer wanted to go home all of a sudden. He brought up a number on his saved list and hit dial.

Tristan answered after three rings. "Hey, what's up?"

"Can we talk?" Hunter said hoarsely.

CHAPTER 25

THEO WALKED THROUGH THE FRONT DOOR OF HIS L.A. villa, grimaced, and rubbed the back of his neck with his good hand. Though he could do more with his injured arm now, he was still having to depend on his employees for a ride and the experience was starting to wear him down.

It'd been different with Hunter. He had looked forward to their drives together and had learned a lot about the man he'd fallen in love with during the time they'd spent in his Jeep.

Theo glanced irritably at his cast. It would be another week before it could come off.

And I'll be glad to see the end of it.

He threw his house keys on the hallway table and walked through the open plan living and dining space of his home to the sliding doors that opened onto the rear of the property. He stepped out onto a terrace framing an infinity pool and overlooking a garden rolling down a gentle slope. The late afternoon sun cast dazzling light across the water. He inhaled deeply and looked out over the hillside of Los Feliz to the hazy Pacific Ocean in the distance.

It had been five days since he'd returned to L.A. to take over running the *Miller* stores in Kate's absence. Though he was glad his business partner was faring better, Theo couldn't suppress his frustration at having had to leave Twilight Falls and Hunter behind so suddenly. He fisted his hands.

God, I miss him.

He and Hunter had talked every single day since they'd parted ways and even had phone sex on a couple of occasions. Theo's dick stirred as he recalled last night's steamy session. He'd given himself a hearty hand job while he watched Hunter play with his cock and his ass on the phone and wished wholeheartedly that he was the one holding the vibrating butt plug Hunter had plunged repeatedly inside his hole until he climaxed.

Hunter's flushed face and pink, twitching ass had occupied Theo's mind most of the day, to the point he'd sported an embarrassing bulge in his pants while he'd been at work.

Theo sighed and headed back inside. He was perusing the contents of his fridge when his intercom buzzed. He straightened, puzzled, and walked over to the video box in the hallway. His pulse jumped when he saw the Jeep outside his gate. He stabbed the answer button wildly with a finger.

"Hunter?!"

"Hey."

Theo's entire body throbbed at the sound of Hunter's voice. "Come in!"

He opened the front door and watched impatiently as Hunter pulled onto his driveway.

Hunter parked next to the porch and stepped out of the vehicle.

"Wow." His gaze roamed Theo's villa. "I knew you were rich, but this place is something else."

Theo stormed down the porch steps, wrapped his good arm around Hunter's waist, and pulled him in for a scorching kiss. Hunter gasped and chuckled before closing his arms around Theo just as tightly, his mouth opening languorously under Theo's demanding tongue.

They were both breathing heavily by the time Theo lifted his mouth from Hunter's.

"Hi," Theo greeted huskily.

Hunter smiled. "I think I said that five minutes ago."

Theo took Hunter's hand and pulled him toward the front door of his home.

"Wait." Hunter removed a backpack from his Jeep and lifted a familiar looking bag from the passenger footwell.

Theo stared. "Is that Chinese takeout?"

Hunter grinned. "Brought to you all the way from Twilight Falls."

They went inside the villa, warmed the dishes up, and spread the meal out over the granite island dominating the kitchen.

"How come you didn't tell me you were gonna visit?" Theo removed a bottle of wine from the cooler and gave it to Hunter.

"Well, it appears I managed to annoy all my friends in

the last five days," Hunter drawled with an amused expression. He opened the bottle, handed a glass to Theo, and took a sip of his drink. "They officially kicked me out of town this weekend and told me to get you out of my system until I was no longer a bona fide asshole."

Theo stared. "What do you mean?"

"The day you left, I got thoroughly wasted at Tristan's place," Hunter confessed, color staining his cheeks. "I think he now knows as much about you as I do, including the exact dimensions of your dick." He grimaced. "I may have drawn him a picture."

Theo choked on his breath.

"I went to Wyatt and Izzy's place the next day. Izzy was the one who suggested the phone sex, by the way, much to Wyatt's eternal embarrassment. That woman could make a porn star blush."

Theo chortled at that.

"Alex and Finn were somewhat bemused when I turned up on their doorstep the following evening." Hunter sighed. "Alex kicked me out when I asked Finn how he liked anal."

Theo burst out laughing.

"Then I went to Drake's place," Hunter continued. "He gave me his homemade whiskey and made me watch a porn video. That guy needs to get out more."

Theo's shoulders shook as he cracked up.

"Luckily for Carter and Elijah, Maisie was still awake when I descended on their home," Hunter said ruefully. "They tolerated my presence until she went to bed and promptly kicked me out. Apparently, the others had already warned them about my visits."

Theo's laughter echoed around the villa. He came over and wrapped his arm around Hunter. "God, I love you!"

HUNTER STIFFENED IN THEO'S HOLD. HIS HEART POUNDED violently in his chest as he looked up at Theo.

"That's the first time you've said that," he said quietly.

Theo's expression softened. "I'm sorry I'm so late." He placed a reverent kiss on Hunter's lips. "I love you, Hunter Thomson. I love you more than life itself."

Hunter's vision grew blurry. He swallowed convulsively, so overfull with emotion he wanted to shout his happiness to the world.

"I love you too, Theo."

This time, Theo's kiss made Hunter's toes practically curl.

They were both panting when Theo lifted his mouth from Hunter's a while later.

"Let's eat," Theo murmured reluctantly.

Hunter nodded tremulously. "Okay."

They talked about what they'd been up to these last few days while they had their meal. Night had fallen by the time Theo led Hunter out to the terrace an hour later.

They sat with their feet dangling in the pool and finished the bottle of wine, the stars blazing brightly above their heads.

"What are we going to do?" Hunter finally said.

Theo gave him a puzzled look.

Hunter took a shallow breath, his innermost fears bubbling to the surface once more.

"I mean about us. You're going to have to come back to L.A. permanently soon."

Theo blinked. "Oh." He put down his glass, carefully lifted Hunter's off him, and laid in on the deck. He took Hunter's hand with his good arm. "About that. I've already spoken to Kate. I'm moving to Twilight Falls once she returns to work."

Shock blazed through Hunter. "What?!"

Theo smiled and nuzzled Hunter's nose with his own. "I still have to come to the city once a week. Codie and I are going to take turns running the *Miller* store in Twilight Falls. He's keen to spend time in our L.A. head office, so the arrangement works perfectly for all of us."

Hunter could only stare. He couldn't believe Theo had given so much thought to their situation already and had come up with a solution that meant they could be together going forward.

"I'm an idiot." Hunter clasped Theo's face with trembling hands and pressed his forehead against Theo's. "Here I was worrying about how we could keep our relationship working long distance and here you were, with it all figured out."

Theo grinned. "I like to have a plan."

Hunter's blood sang with love as he gazed at the man before him. "What have I done to deserve you?"

Theo's expression turned serious. "That's my line." He pressed a gentle kiss to Hunter's mouth and hugged Hunter tightly. "I'm so glad I decided to follow you to that restroom in L.A."

Hunter smiled against Theo's shoulder. "Wait. You

followed me?" He pulled back and almost laughed out loud at Theo's guilty grimace.

"Busted," Theo mumbled.

Happiness filled Hunter once more. He knew then that he and Theo would be okay. That they would be together for a long, long time. He could sense it in the way Theo was looking at him and in Theo's gentle touch.

Desire pooled inside Hunter's belly. The raw sexual tension that had been simmering between them since he stepped out of his Jeep heated his body up.

"Have I ever told you about that time I went skinny dipping in the river?"

CHAPTER 26

Theo's cock throbbed painfully at Hunter's sultry words. He followed Hunter hungrily with his gaze as Hunter rose to his feet, stripped out of his clothes, and dove smoothly into the deep end of the pool.

He's going to be the death of me.

Hunter swam the length of the pool smoothly, the soft lights around the bottom highlighting his strong, toned body as he moved under the water toward where Theo still sat at the shallow end. He came up for air a few feet away and smiled teasingly when he spied the unmistakable bulge of Theo's arousal, droplets gleaming enticingly on his wet hair and skin.

"Enjoying the show?" Hunter said as he treaded water.

Theo's gaze dropped to Hunter's swelling dick beneath the choppy surface.

"Very much so. It's a shame I can't join you."

Hunter glanced at Theo's cast. "I gotta say, I can't wait for that to come off." He moved closer. "How about I make it up to you another way?"

Theo shivered when Hunter placed his hands on his thighs and spread them wide. Hunter undid the top button of Theo's pants, leaned in, and grabbed the zipper with his teeth.

The erotic sound of the metal being unfastened and the lustful look Hunter gave him from under his eyelashes as he pulled it down had Theo's belly clenching in anticipation. His erection sprang free a moment later.

Hunter wasted little time giving Theo what he wanted. He played Theo's shaft expertly with his clever fingers and tongue until Theo was groaning, before taking his quivering member inside his mouth.

Theo braced his good hand on the deck and dropped his head back as Hunter started blowing him, pleasure sending red pulses throbbing across his vision, his breaths leaving his throat in harsh gasps and grunts. He would never tire of this wicked feeling. Of Hunter's hands. His lips. His tongue. Of the way Hunter caressed and sucked him like he couldn't get enough of his cock.

Theo's climax came too soon and he emptied his seed inside Hunter's throat with a fierceness that made him shudder from his head all the way to his toes. He opened his eyes after a long, earth shattering moment and looked down into Hunter's flushed face, blood still pounding dully in his skull.

"Come here."

Hunter's dick trembled at Theo's gravelly voice.

He licked his lips and climbed out of the pool, the taste of Theo's cum still heavy on his tongue.

Theo took Hunter's hand and pulled him inside the villa.

Hunter's heart thrummed against his ribcage as Theo guided him down a light and airy corridor to a large bedroom with views over L.A.

Theo fetched a towel from the bathroom and dried Hunter thoroughly, his touch hot and firm. Neither of them spoke, the only sound in the room that of their ragged breathing.

Theo undressed, dropped featherlight kisses on Hunter's throat and chest, and pushed him down on the bed.

Hunter's eyes widened when Theo opened the top drawer of his nightstand and removed several items from inside. He pushed up on his elbows and stared, his gaze skimming the condoms and lube to focus firmly on a purple vibrator.

Hunter's ass quivered as he studied its enticing length and girth.

"Do you like it?" Theo dented the mattress with a knee and climbed on the bed.

"When did you get that?" Hunter murmured.

"I bought it two days ago." A dirty smile curved Theo's mouth. "I was planning to bring it back with me this weekend and use it on you."

"I like it. A lot." Hunter's gaze shifted to Theo's groin. He chewed his lower lip. "But I gotta say, I like the idea of your dick inside me better."

Theo groaned, his swelling cock growing bigger and

harder under Hunter's hungry stare. "I'm trying to be patient and gentle here."

A sexy smile split Hunter's mouth. "Don't worry." He parted his thighs and dropped a hand to his hole. "I prepped myself with the butt plug before I came here tonight, so I'm nice and loose already."

THEO CURSED AT HUNTER'S WICKEDLY WANTON WORDS AND the way he teased the pink folds of his entrance. He wrapped his good hand around Hunter's nape and took his mouth in a passionate kiss.

I can't believe he's really mine.

Hunter moaned softly when Theo pushed his tongue past his lips and wrapped his hot flesh around his. Theo maneuvered Hunter onto his back, settled in the cradle of Hunter's thighs, and started making his way down Hunter's body, fingers busy on Hunter's nipples while his lips, tongue, and teeth worked Hunter's hot skin.

Hunter trembled and twitched as Theo sucked and nipped at his chest and six-pack. He gasped when Theo circled his belly button with his tongue before trailing the wet tip down his tense abdomen to his groin.

Theo kissed Hunter's swollen cock before massaging Hunter's balls and taking them inside his mouth.

"Ah!"

Hunter closed his eyes tight and clutched the pillow behind his head, his hips bucking off the mattress. He reached down blindly with one hand and grasped Theo's head, his thighs dropping wide open to accommodate Theo better.

Theo obeyed his silent plea and finally took his cock in his mouth.

Hunter gasped and keened softly as Theo started blowing him hard and deep, his wicked lips dragging enticingly along Hunter's shaft while he wrapped his strong tongue around Hunter's sensitive flesh.

The snap of the bottle of lube being opened reached Hunter dimly. A lustful hiss escaped him when Theo rubbed his pucker with a wet thumb.

"Yesss!"

Hunter lost track of time as Theo sucked his cock and prepped his ass, his orgasm building in slow, tantalizing waves that had him undulating sensuously on the bed. He buried his fingers in Theo's hair and dug his heels in Theo's strong shoulders, his touch demanding.

Theo gave him what he wanted and more, his heated pants filling the room as he feasted on Hunter's erection and loosened Hunter's hole.

Hunter came with a loud shout when Theo thrust a third finger inside him, his hips pumping uncontrollably as he shoved his jerking cock deep into the back of Theo's throat. Theo moved his fingers briskly in and out Hunter's body while he gulped and swallowed Hunter's cum, his feral grunts vibrating through Hunter's aching flesh.

By the time Theo removed his hand from Hunter's ass and replaced it with the head of the lubed up vibrator, Hunter was sweating profusely and his spent dick was swelling with a fresh wave of arousal.

Theo knelt between Hunter's thighs, hooked Hunter's legs around his waist, and pressed the sex toy gently home, his face flushed and his eyes dark with desire.

Hunter rose up on his elbows and watched breathlessly as his body slowly opened up and swallowed the slicked-up rubber shaft. A stinging sensation throbbed through his hole when the broad head of the toy stretched the band of muscles guarding his passage.

This was the thickest toy they'd used so far during sex to get Hunter accustomed to the act of penetration.

"Breathe out," Theo instructed softly. "Relax, Hunter."

Hunter inhaled shallowly and did as he was told, forcing his lower body and his hole to unclench. The tight ring spasmed and opened a moment later.

The vibrator slid in smoothly and started filling him up.

Hunter bit his lip at the strange new sensation. He squeezed his ass tentatively. A bolt of insane pleasure shot through him as his back passage grasped the intruder within.

"Oh God!"

"Shit," Theo mumbled.

Hunter met Theo's wild gaze as Theo steadily pushed the vibrator all the way up his ass. They both stilled when the toy was fully nestled inside him.

Theo leaned down and kissed Hunter. "You okay?"

Hunter nodded shakily. He felt hot and full and aching down there.

A startled cry left him when Theo pressed one of the buttons on the sex toy, causing it to vibrate. Hunter whimpered at the electric tingles shooting through his body from his back passage. His inner muscles clenched instinctively around the thick rubber shaft, squeezing and relaxing in a rhythm that mimicked the act of sex.

"Theo!" Hunter moaned.

"Yes?"

Hunter grabbed Theo's wrist where he held the vibrator. *"Move!"*

Theo growled and gave in to Hunter's desperate plea.

Hunter's cock leaked and pulsed precum as Theo withdrew and shoved the lubed up love stick repeatedly through his throbbing hole. He cried out and bowed his spine off the bed when the broad head of the vibrator massaged his prostate, his breath locking in his throat at the waves of intense pleasure surging through his body.

Hunter came all too soon, his climax so powerful he shot cum all the way up his chest and onto his neck.

Theo leaned down and kissed the musky essence off his skin. Hunter moaned when Theo withdrew the sex toy from his back passage.

"Did you enjoy that?" Theo ran his tongue teasingly inside the whirls of Hunter's left ear.

Hunter shivered and nodded wordlessly, his chest heaving with his breaths and his heart thundering against his rib cage. His mind was a haze and his body limp with pleasure.

"Good," Theo murmured. "Because the next thing going inside your ass is my dick."

CHAPTER 27

Hunter's pleasure-dazed eyes darkened at Theo's filthy words.

Theo swallowed a groan at the desire burning in the gray depths. He would never forget tonight for as long as he lived.

The way Hunter had entrusted his body to him.

The way he'd shown no fear as Theo prepared his body for what was to come.

The way he'd already climaxed twice from having his ass played with.

Theo couldn't wait to be inside Hunter's body and make him come all over again. He sheathed his trembling shaft with a condom, poured lube over it liberally, and yanked Hunter up.

"Ride me," Theo said thickly at Hunter's startled expression. "It'll be easier for you to control the penetration."

Hunter's pupils dilated. He nodded shakily.

Theo propped up a couple of pillows, laid down on the bed, and watched as Hunter straddled his lower body.

Hunter rocked his hips slowly.

Theo groaned as the motion caused his straining erection to rub Hunter's butt.

A wicked smile curved Hunter's mouth. He reached behind and slid Theo's dick through his hot crack.

Theo hissed. "You're such a tease!" He bucked his hips up.

Hunter chuckled. His smile faded as he pressed his hands on Theo's chest, dug his heels in the bed, and lifted his body over Theo's raging member.

They both stared breathlessly to where Hunter squatted and guided Theo's erection to his hole.

Hunter dropped his head back and moaned sexily as he rubbed his pucker across the head of Theo's cock.

Theo bit his lip and grunted, keeping himself still by a sheer act of will.

All he wanted to do was to shove his hips up, drive his dick inside Hunter, and find his release.

Hunter's breathing stuttered as he pressed down slowly onto Theo's shaft. He tilted his head forward and locked his burning gaze with Theo's as Theo penetrated his body.

Theo stilled when his cock met the stiff band of muscles protecting Hunter's back passage.

Hunter inhaled shallowly, sweat dripping off his nose and splashing hotly on Theo's belly. Theo felt the tight ring gradually relax as Hunter concentrated on his breathing. He pushed up slightly.

Hunter gasped and froze.

Theo froze. "Are you okay?"

Hunter nodded tremulously. "It feels," a low hum left him, "—*fuck,* I can't describe it!"

Though Hunter couldn't put words to what he was feeling, Theo could tell that it had everything to do with pleasure and little to do with pain. He thrust gently once more.

Hunter let out a lustful sound as Theo's dick slipped through the final barrier and slowly filled his ass. His fingers clenched on Theo's chest as he drove his hips down and took Theo to the hilt.

They stayed still and breathed heavily as Hunter's butt rested snugly on Theo's groin.

"You're inside me," Hunter said, his expression somewhat stunned.

"I sure am," Theo said with a strained chuckle.

Hunter gasped and closed his eyes. "Ah! I felt that."

He rocked his hips.

Theo groaned when the motion caused his erection to move inside Hunter. Pleasure throbbed through his belly.

Hunter squirmed and shuddered above Theo as he tried out different angles of taking him. He found one that he liked, held on to Theo's chest, and lifted his ass tentatively up Theo's shaft.

Theo felt the head of his cock nudge the soft bump of Hunter's prostate as Hunter pushed back down again.

They both cursed out loud.

"*Oh yeah!*" Hunter gasped. He rolled his hips until he found his rhythm and started impaling himself lustily on Theo's rock hard cock, his pink pucker spasming and dragging hungrily on Theo's shaft. "Fuck that feels good!"

Theo couldn't agree more. He dug his heels in the mattress, grasped Hunter's right thigh with his good hand, and met his downward thrusts with strong, rolling motions of his hips, the bolts of pleasure shooting through his dick and balls so intense he could only grunt.

Hunter was so hot and tight, it was a miracle he hadn't exploded the minute he entered him.

Hunter's cries of pleasure grew louder as he neared his climax.

"*Oh! Oh God!*" He gazed dazedly at Theo, his movements growing frenzied as he rammed his hole repeatedly on Theo's shaft. "I'm coming! *Theo!*"

Theo gnashed his teeth when Hunter's back passage contracted painfully around his erection. A guttural noise left Hunter. He stiffened above Theo for a timeless moment, his face and chest flushing with color as his orgasm hit him, the muscles and tendons in his neck taut with tension. Breathless sounds left him as he convulsed sensuously above Theo, hips writhing and cock pulsing out cum onto Theo's belly and six-pack, his ass squeezing Theo's dick hungrily.

The first wave of Theo's climax stormed through him when he met Hunted's pleasure-glazed eyes. He growled and grunted as he pinned Hunter's hips in place with a powerful hand and pounded Hunter's hole with his raging erection. A buzzing noise filled his ears.

Theo shouted lustily as he came, the sound echoing around the bedroom.

Hunter shivered and moaned as Theo exploded violently inside him, his strong white teeth biting down sexily on his lower lip as his ass stretched to accommodate the rapidly filling condom.

Blood pounded dully in Theo's head when he finally relaxed down on the bed, his softening cock still wedged deep inside Hunter.

"Wow," Hunter mumbled.

Theo sat up and tugged Hunter's head toward him for a long, sultry kiss.

"So, what's it like getting your cherry properly popped, Mr. Thomson?" he panted against Hunter's lips.

Hunter's eyes sparkled opposite Theo. "It felt fucking sublime, Mr. Miller."

Theo chuckled.

Hunter groaned.

"Wait," he mumbled a few seconds later. "Are you—?"

Theo rocked his hips gently. "Hard again? Yup."

Hunter buried his face in Theo's neck. "Christ, at least give me a minute to recover."

Theo laughed and pressed a kiss on Hunter's hair. "We have all the time in the world."

CHAPTER 28

"I don't know whether to be happy or annoyed at how smug you look right now," Izzy said moodily.

Hunter blinked at her innocently. "I have no idea what you mean."

"She's right," Wyatt muttered. "You're practically glowing."

Hunter stifled a grin.

They were having coffee in *La Petite Bouche Gourmande* after closing hours. Elijah finished cleaning up in the kitchen and joined them.

"Is Theo coming back tonight?"

Hunter nodded. This time, he was unable to contain his smile of happiness. His friends stared.

"Like the goddamn sun," Izzy grumbled.

Two weeks had passed since Hunter had gone to L.A. to see Theo.

They'd spent the weekend making passionate love and planning Theo's eventual move to Twilight Falls. Hunter had visited Kate with Theo before he left L.A. and they'd all approved of Theo's idea to let Codie use his villa when the store manager was in town.

Hunter had yet to tell his friends about the monumental decision he and Theo had made concerning their future. He was hoping both he and Theo would give them the news tonight.

Izzy stabbed her cake with a fork and waved a frosted piece at Hunter.

"So what happened? You finally got your cherry popped by Theo or something?"

Hunter felt his ears grow warm.

Tristan's spoon clanged on his saucer where it fell from his grasp. He gazed pale-faced at Hunter.

"It's okay," Hunter said reassuringly. "I'm fine."

"I'd say you're more than fine," Izzy said tartly.

Drake grinned. "Our little boy is all grown up."

Hunter rolled his eyes. "You know you're only two months older than me, right?"

The bakery door jangled open. Alex and Finn walked in.

"What'd we miss?" Alex said breezily as he pulled a couple of chairs over.

"Hunter slept with Theo," Elijah announced. "As in, they went all the way."

Alex raised an eyebrow. "So, how was it?"

Hunter's mouth split in a wide smile.

Alex chuckled. "You lucky, lucky bastard."

"I'm standing right next to you," Finn said with an affronted expression.

Alex kissed his husband. "I'm a lucky bastard too."

Finn's frown melted away.

Carter arrived shortly with Maisie in tow. “So, what are we celebrating?” he asked curiously while Elijah fetched more cake and a lemonade for Maisie.

Izzy narrowed her eyes at Hunter. “Apart from admitting that he and Theo have finally consumated their relationship, pretty boy over there hasn’t said anything yet.”

“What does consumate mean, Aunt Izzy?” Maisie said innocently.

Izzy’s eyes widened. She opened and closed her mouth soundlessly.

“That one’s on you,” Carter stated without a trace of pity.

“You brought this on yourself,” Wyatt agreed with a nod.

The noise of a familiar engine reached Hunter’s ears, distracting him from the guys teasing Izzy. He looked outside just as a car pulled up next to the bakery.

Hunter’s pulse skittered when Theo climbed out of the Jag. His lover looked cool and sexy in gray linen pants, an open-neck shirt, and a blue blazer.

It was three days since Theo’s cast had come off and five days since they’d last seen one another.

“Here comes the man of the hour,” Izzy drawled as Theo walked in.

Theo greeted Hunter’s friends and dropped a warm kiss on Hunter’s mouth as he took the seat beside him.

“So, you guys are finally going to tell us what it is Hunter is so excited about?” Alex asked after Elijah served more coffee and cake.

Hunter hesitated before taking Theo’s hand and gazing at his friends, suddenly nervous.

These were the people he cared most for in the world and having their blessing meant a lot to him. Miles's face flashed before his eyes then and brought with it a wave of bittersweet emotion.

Theo squeezed Hunter's fingers reassuringly.

"Theo is moving to Twilight Falls," Hunter announced. "And he'll be living with me."

Silence fell across the room.

"We know." Izzy glanced at the others. "Imogen spilled the beans a week ago."

"*What?!*" Hunter squealed after a shocked pause.

"I mean, we were kind of expecting it," Drake said with a shrug.

"We even planned a welcome party and everything," Carter added.

This earned him a battery of frowns and two stunned stares.

Elijah sighed. "That was meant to be a surprise, babe."

Carter's face fell. "Oh."

Maisie giggled.

Hunter's heart thudded in his chest as he gazed at his friends.

"You're all okay with this?" he mumbled.

"Why wouldn't we be?" Izzy said drily. "It's obvious how much you two care for each other." She arched an eyebrow. "So, do I sense another wedding on the horizon?"

Hunter flushed, flustered. "We haven't spoken about—"

"Spring," Theo said quietly. "I've always wanted a spring wedding."

Hunter gazed into Theo's eyes, not sure whether to be shocked or deliriously happy at what he read deep in the hazel depths opposite him.

"Are—are you asking me to marry you?" Hunter stammered.

Theo nuzzled his nose. "I am." He smiled faintly and glanced around the table. "I can't think of a better time than this."

Hunter swallowed convulsively, his stomach a jumble of knots.

"Hurry it up, Hunter," Izzy groaned.

"Yeah, the suspense is killing us," Carter muttered.

Hunter blinked rapidly, his eyes wet with tears.

"Yes," he breathed.

The whole room exploded with applause and loud hoots.

"I think that means I'm officially part of your family now." Theo grinned and pressed his lips to Hunter's temple, his gaze full of love.

"So, how good are you at poker?" Alex said once the noise had died down, his expression turning serious. "We need to trash Tristan."

Tristan rolled his eyes hard, much to Maisie's amusement.

Dusk was falling when Hunter and Theo drove onto their estate later that day.

Theo climbed out of his car and took Hunter's hand as they climbed the steps to Hunter's place. By the time they made it to the bedroom, they'd already half undressed.

Hunter flicked the light on the nightstand while Theo yanked his jeans and boxers off his legs. He chuckled when Theo cursed, fingers fumbling on the buttons of his own pants.

"Want me to get that for you?" Hunter murmured, nibbling on Theo's throat. He lowered his hands and covered Theo's fingers.

Theo groaned and let him take over.

They kissed and stroked each other's cocks for long minutes before moving to the bed. Hunter wrenched his lips from Theo's mouth and removed a bottle of lube from the nightstand drawer.

"Oh." Theo paused where he was busy fondling Hunter's erection. "Want me to grab some condoms from my place?"

Hunter shook his head, surprised at his own boldness.

"No condoms. I want to have sex with you bare tonight."

Theo cursed as Hunter caressed his hard shaft and leaned down to kiss the head of his cock.

CHAPTER 29

THEO'S HEART SLAMMED AGAINST HIS RIBS WHEN HUNTER pushed him to sit against the headboard. Hunter spread Theo's thighs and settled on his knees between Theo's stretched out legs.

"How about you relax and let me do some of the hard work?" Hunter said in a low, teasing voice.

He probed Theo's mouth with his tongue, frenched Theo for long, delicious seconds, and started making love to him with his hands and lips and tongue.

Theo groaned and twitched as Hunter lavished his body with hot kisses and scorching touches. By the time Hunter went on all fours and took Theo's leaking dick inside his mouth, Theo was close to climaxing.

He grabbed the bottle of lube, poured a generous amount in his palm, and reached down Hunter's back. He slid his fingers down Hunter's crack and touched and massaged Hunter's pucker.

Hunter grunted where he was busy bobbing his head on Theo's erection, the throaty sound causing Theo to curse. Hunter's movements became jerky when Theo slipped one, then two fingers inside his hole. He panted and moaned as he hollowed his cheeks and took Theo all the way to the back of his throat.

Theo closed his eyes, pleasure coursing through him in growing waves that tightened his balls and belly.

Hunter grazed Theo's cock lightly with his teeth.

Theo's breath locked in his throat. A guttural sound escaped him as his orgasm swept over him. He thrust his hips wildly into Hunter's mouth while he continued plundering Hunter's ass with his fingers.

Hunter sucked and licked Theo until he'd swallowed every last drop of his cum, his gaze hooded and his face flushed with passion where he looked at Theo from beneath his lashes.

"Come here," Theo ordered thickly.

He pulled Hunter up onto his knees, gripped his hips, and closed his mouth around his erection.

Hunter moaned sexily as Theo started blowing him. He gasped when Theo spread his thighs and probed his entrance once more.

Theo fucked Hunter with his fingers and sucked his cock until he came, his cries of pleasure resonating loudly in Theo's ears. Hunter was still shuddering from his powerful orgasm when Theo turned him around, forced him onto his hands and knees, and crowded his back, his movements rough and frantic with need.

Theo grabbed his fresh arousal in one hand and parted Hunter's butt cheeks with the other.

HUNTER'S BREATH STUTTERED WHEN HE FELT THEO TEASE his slick opening. Theo's bare cock was hot and hard where he rubbed it against Hunter's hole.

Hunter groaned at the sublime sensation.

He dropped his head and panted when Theo started pushing in. "*Oh!*"

Theo's dick stretched Hunter's ass deliciously as he entered him in slow thrusts.

"*Ah!*" they both hissed when Theo reached the tightest part of him.

Theo reached around and closed a hand on Hunter's twitching dick.

Hunter whimpered as Theo started stroking him, pulses of pleasure shooting through his body from Theo's hot fingers and where his stiff member was partly wedged inside him.

"*Shit!*" Hunter gasped. "You're driving me crazy!"

Theo pressed his lips to the hot stretch of skin between Hunter's shoulder blades.

"You're so tight!" he growled. "Your ass is the best thing my cock has ever tasted!"

Theo sank his teeth in Hunter's flesh.

"Oh God!" Hunter cried out.

His back passage contracted and relaxed at the savage love bite.

Theo grunted and slid home in a single deep thrust that saw him lodged in all the way to the hilt.

They stilled at the filthy, earthy sensation of their first bareback lovemaking, Theo's heart thundering against Hunter's back where he pressed his chest snugly to Hunter.

"Theo," Hunter begged after a breathless moment. *"Please!"*

He wiggled his butt against Theo's groin, drawing a groan from both of them.

Theo nibbled on Hunter's nape. "Tell me what you want, Hunter. I want to hear you say the words."

Heat flooded Hunter's face at Theo's commanding voice.

"I want you to fuck me," he breathed. "Take me, Theo. Pound my hole with your cock."

An animal sound left Theo. He grabbed Hunter's hips in a punishing grip, withdrew his erection from Hunter's body, and slammed right back in.

Stars exploded across Hunter's vision. He shouted and arched his back.

The bed creaked as Theo gave Hunter exactly what he'd asked for, thrusting hard and deep.

Hunter's knuckles whitened where he gripped the bedsheets, body rocking to and fro with the power of Theo's penetration.

Theo looped one arm around Hunter's waist and closed a hand on Hunter's left hand, twining their fingers together. His heated breaths raised goosebumps on Hunter's skin as he grunted and panted against Hunter's back.

It didn't take long for Theo to take them both over the edge.

Hunter closed his eyes tight and bit his lip as Theo's cock swelled and exploded inside him, stunned by how exquisite it felt to have his lover spill his seed in the forbidden depths of his body. Theo's cum stretched his passage to the brim as he continued thrusting, making him even more wet and hot.

Hunter was still panting and moaning when Theo pulled out, flipped him onto his back, and yanked his legs around his waist. Desire throbbed through Hunter as he took in Theo's feverish expression and still rock hard cock.

Theo plunged straight back inside him, his face flushed and sweat dripping off his nose as he rolled his hips and fucked Hunter again.

Hunter's feet found purchase against the headboard. He rolled his body off the bed and met Theo's demanding thrusts, his fingers twisting in the bedsheets.

"Theo! Theo!"

"So good!" Theo groaned. "Fuck, Hunter! It feels so *good* inside you!"

Theo's movements became frenzied as he neared his climax.

Hunter gasped and groaned as Theo rammed his cock harder and deeper inside him, Theo's erection probing Hunter's prostate over and over again. He came seconds before Theo, his passage contracting sweetly around the stiff intruder plunging inside the hot depths of his body, his stiff cock spurting out cum onto his clenching belly.

Theo's savage shout of pleasure echoed in Hunter's ears a moment later.

His hips pumped fitfully against Hunter's hole and his fingers bit punishingly in Hunter's waist as he groaned and came powerfully inside him, his hot seed pulsing out and filling Hunter's back passage.

Hunter locked his legs around Theo's hips and kept

him prisoner as Theo huffed and continued thrusting, unable to control the rocking motion of his body.

"Theo," Hunter moaned, his ass squeezing and milking Theo's cock lovingly.

Theo leaned down and kissed him passionately before pushing him on the bed and collapsing atop him.

Hunter wrapped trembling arms around Theo as Theo panted against him, face buried in Hunter's throat.

"That was amazing," Theo mumbled after a while.

"Yeah?" Hunter breathed.

Theo raised his head and kissed the tip of Hunter's nose.

"I will never get enough of you."

Hunter's heart swelled with emotion at Theo's burning gaze.

Something else swelled inside him.

Hunter groaned. "You cannot be hard again."

Theo chuckled.

Hunter moaned as the motion caused Theo's arousal to rub his insides.

"How about we take this to the bathroom?" Theo said throatily, his voice making Hunter tremble all over again.

Hunter sucked in air when Theo slowly pulled out of his body. He flushed in the next instant as sticky wetness oozed out of him.

Theo's eyes blazed with untamed desire as he gently touched Hunter's pleasantly swollen pucker and fingered his hole.

"Let's clean you out first," he growled.

Theo climbed off the bed, leaned down, and lifted a shocked Hunter over his shoulder.

Hunter chuckled shakily. "I think your caveman side is showing."

Theo patted Hunter's butt lovingly as he walked into the bathroom. "You ain't seen nothing yet. I'll show you exactly what this caveman can do."

Hunter's cock throbbed with fresh arousal at Theo's wicked threat.

And show him Theo did. In the shower. In the bedroom.

And pretty much all around the house.

Thank you for reading HUNTER!
I hope you loved this third book in TWILIGHT FALLS.
Want to know when Wyatt's story will be released? Sign-up to my newsletter to find out. You will also get an EXCLUSIVE FREE ebook as a thank you for being part of my reader group and news about sales and giveaways.

➤ https://www.amsalinger.com/iwyv

You can also join my VIP Facebook Fan Group for exclusive sneak peeks at my upcoming books:

➤ https://www.amsalinger.com/o5dz

If you enjoyed HUNTER, please consider leaving a review on your favorite book site. Reviews help readers find books!

Have you read the NIGHTS series yet? Turn the page to read an extract from ONE NIGHT (NIGHTS #1) and find out if Gabe Anderson accepts Cam Sorvino's promise of one night of mindless pleasure to help him overcome his phobia of intimacy!

ONE NIGHT (NIGHTS #1) SPECIAL PREVIEW

CHAPTER 1

What the hell am I doing here?

Gabe Anderson scanned the crowded club in the mirror opposite the bar before looking down into his scotch with a self-deprecating smile. This had seemed like such a great idea an hour ago, when he'd been staring at an empty weekend in an even emptier apartment.

Saron was located in a side alley, a short walk from Shinjuku's main club strip. Despite its somewhat shady location, the place oozed style.

Gabe had hesitated when he'd seen the suited doorman guarding the entrance and wondered if access was by invitation only. He only knew of *Saron* from overhearing his clients mention it a few nights ago. From what he'd made of their excited conversation, it was *the* place to hang out in Shinjuku if you were of a particular sexual inclination.

The doorman had checked Gabe over for all of three seconds before wordlessly unclipping the rope from the stanchions framing the steel doors. He had obviously passed some kind of test, though what it was he didn't know.

Beyond a foyer with a cloakroom manned by a male attendant who looked like he'd walked straight out of a *GQ* shoot were a set of shallow steps leading to a wide, sunken floor.

Despite the butterflies churning his stomach, Gabe had stopped and stared appreciatively at the decor. As a consultant for one of Chicago's biggest design firms, he could tell how much money had gone into giving *Saron* its unique look. The club was drowned in deep reds, dark purples, and rich earth tones. Scattered across the oak floor were Brazilian cherry wood tables and armchairs boasting plush velvet upholstery and satin cushions. Discrete booths dotted the walls and afforded privacy to those who needed it, although the muted lighting provided enough of that as it was. A polished mahogany counter with wine-red leather and walnut stools ran the length of the bar on the right.

At the far end of the room, a woman in a black cocktail dress stood on a raised podium. She was crooning a song in a sultry, deep voice, her eyes closed and her glossy ruby lips glistening in the mellow spotlight. Behind her, cymbals vibrated gently, a piano tinkled, and a saxophone hummed, the sounds somehow rising above the voices of the men packing the place.

It was as he'd made his way to the bar that Gabe had realized why the doorman had let him in. From the looks of the club's patrons, *Saron* catered exclusively to an upscale clientele. He was willing to bet a week's wages none of the suits in the place cost less than five hundred dollars.

"Ah, fresh meat."

Gabe froze in the act of sitting on a barstool, his gaze swinging up to meet a pair of amused green eyes on the other side of the mahogany counter.

"Excuse me?" he said stiffly.

The bartender, a striking blond in a slate, silk tuxedo vest and crisp white shirt, flashed him a grin.

"I've not seen you around these parts before. What will it be?"

Gabe swallowed, wondering whether the man had seen straight through him and grasped the reason he had come to *Saron*.

"What will what be?" he mumbled, unable to mask the apprehension in his voice.

The bartender pursed his lips and observed him with a shrewd expression before leaning across the counter.

"Relax," he murmured in Gabe's left ear. "I can tell it's your first time in a place like this. If you keep up that deer-in-the-headlights look you've got painted across that pretty face of yours, you're gonna be a target for every sleaze ball in this club. And, trust me, they might be wearing thousand-dollar ensembles, but some of these assholes are nothing but dirty pigs in suits."

An involuntary bark of laughter left Gabe's lips at the mental image the bartender's words had conjured. The sound carried along the counter, drawing stares.

The knot of tension that had been sitting between

Gabe's shoulder blades ever since he ventured into Shinjuku eased as he smiled at the bartender.

"I've never been called pretty before."

The guy winked.

"Trust me, you're the hottest thing on legs in this place right now. Besides me, of course."

Gabe chuckled and ordered a scotch, his confidence boosted by the compliment.

Two months had passed since he'd relocated to Tokyo from Chicago. When his bosses had sprung the offer on Gabe in early spring, the chance of a fresh start in a place void of the dark memories that had plagued him for eight years was too much of an attractive proposition for him to reject. He'd left Chicago with two suitcases and five crates full of books and artwork, the only things he had to show after a decade in the city.

Though he had been prepared for the culture shock, life in Tokyo had still come as a surprise, albeit an invigorating one. He had always had an interest in the country and its intoxicating mix of traditional and contemporary customs ever since he made his first business trip to the Japanese branch of the firm four years ago.

Luckily, his new position suited him to a T. He had thrown himself into his first assignment with his usual drive and passion, leading the team under him to make good on a project, one which his predecessor had only made a half-assed attempt to complete. He had delivered on time, on budget, and on schedule, despite the nearly impossible deadline. The crazy hours and weekends he had put in had not gone unnoticed, and the praise lavished on his team at the grand opening of their client's luxury hotel earlier that week was all the acknowledgment Gabe needed to realize he had made the right choice in moving to this city. The fact that the money he was making could easily afford him a two-bedroom condo in the exclusive neighborhood of Meguro didn't hurt, either.

Yet, despite having relocated thousands of miles to the other side of the world, his mind would not let go of the bite of his past. Which was why, when faced with the prospect of his first free weekend and the boxes he had yet to unpack, he had looked up *Saron*'s location on the spur of the moment and decided to take a gamble.

He had promised himself this move would not be just a fresh start for his mind, but for his body, too. That he would start taking risks in his personal life again. That he would not let the bastard who had made it impossible for him to ever have a satisfying physical relationship win.

Fifteen minutes into his first drink and Gabe wondered whether he had made a bad choice. So far, Ethan, the bartender, had helped him field a burly, yakuza-looking type with tattoos up the side of his neck, three old men with sweaty palms and bald patches, and a couple of young guys who looked barely past the legal age of drinking.

With his lean build, dark hair, and blue eyes, Gabe knew he was an attractive prospect. Add in that he was a foreigner and he was coming to the conclusion that he had become a beeline for all the men in the bar who wanted to make a conquest out of the white guy – a white notch in the proverbial bedpost. They all wanted to fuck him or be fucked by him.

A cynical half-smile twisted his lips at that thought. If only they knew.

He raised a hand to the back of his neck and rubbed the warm spot that had been bothering him for a while. Something made him look up from his drink then – call it instinct or that subconscious voice that warns of imminent danger. Movement in the mirror opposite the bar caught his gaze. Or, more precisely, a lack of it.

Stormy gray eyes pierced him from the other end of the club. They locked on him, a beam of light in the gloom. Transfixing him. Immobilizing him.

Gabe's breath caught in his throat, every muscle in his body tightening in fight-or-flight mode.

The man sat apart from the crowd, alone at a table that could have accommodated three, a tumbler full of dark liquid clasped casually in his left hand. His red silk tie was crooked, as if he had slipped a finger through the knot to loosen it. The top two buttons on his white shirt were open, revealing tan skin covering toned muscles and a hint of curls.

Gabe couldn't tell whether his hair was dark brown or dirty blond. It was hard to say in the dim light. What wasn't hard to see were the subtle and not-so-subtle stares the other men in the bar were giving the stranger.

With his stubbled face, smoldering looks, and what appeared to be an incredibly ripped body beneath a custom-tailored charcoal suit, the man looked like a king sitting on a throne, commanding a roomful of servants. Servants who appeared more than willing to either get fucked by him or fuck him if he so much as lifted his little finger.

And a man like that would not have to ask twice.

Envy and irritation flashed through Gabe at that thought, shattering the spell he found himself under. He broke eye contact, shocked by the feelings suddenly flooding him, and glared at his half-empty glass. It seemed to mock him, as if it were a reflection of his own life. A half-empty, broken shell. Incapable of touching someone or to be touched.

Gabe lifted the glass and downed the rest of the drink with an angry flick of his wrist. Fire singed his throat. He welcomed the burning sensation, hoping it would calm the pounding in his chest and the tightness in his belly and groin that told him his body had reacted to the stranger.

A full glass of scotch appeared next to his empty tumbler.

Gabe looked up at Ethan, puzzled.

A remorseful grimace flashed across the bartender's face. "Looks like we're no longer the two hottest bastards in this joint. Here, compliments of the King."

Gabe stared at the drink before slowly looking over his shoulder, his pulse picking up speed.

Gray Eyes raised his glass in a toast. A teasing smile played on his sculptured lips before he knocked back his drink.

You're kidding me.

Gabe tried to block out the heated tingle running across his skin at the stranger's cocky smirk and the way his powerful throat muscles worked when he swallowed. He turned to Ethan.

"That's his *actual* name?"

Ethan grunted. "Well, no. But the asshole sure acts like one."

There was movement in the mirror opposite Gabe.

➤ GET ONE NIGHT NOW!

BOOKS BY A.M. SALINGER

NIGHTS

One Night (Nights #1)

The Escort (Nights #2)

Tokyo Heat (Nights #3)

Sweet Obsession (Nights #4)

Sweet Possession (Nights #5)

The Proposition (Nights #6)

Undisclosed (Nights #7)

Hush (Nights #8)

One Day (Nights #9)

TWILIGHT FALLS

Alex (Twilight Falls #1)

Carter (Twilight Falls #2)

Hunter (Twilight Falls #3)

COMING SOON...

Wyatt (Twilight Falls #4)

Join my mailing list to find out about my upcoming releases and to get a FREE exclusive ebook. You can also join my VIP FB Group for exclusive excerpts of what I'm working on right now!

➤ READER GROUP

➤ AVA'S NIGHTS CLUB

ABOUT THE AUTHOR

Ava Marie Salinger is the pen name of an Amazon bestselling fantasy author who has always wanted to write scorching hot contemporary and erotic romance. In 2017, she finally decided to venture to the steamy side. NIGHTS is the first of several sizzling series featuring sweet, sexy men with dark pasts and a whole lot of love to give to the ones brave enough to fight for their hearts. When she's not dreaming up hotties to write about, you'll find Ava creating kickass music playlists to write to, spying on the wildlife in her garden, drooling over gadgets, and eating Chinese.

Here are some other places where you can connect with her:

www.amsalinger.com
Ava's Nights Club

CPSIA information can be obtained
at www.ICGtesting.com
Printed in the USA
LVHW050106240620
658806LV00011B/1440